W9-BUY-533

Also by William Allen

————————

Starkweather

To Tojo from Billy-Bob Jones

THE FIRE IN
THE BIRDBATH

and Other Disturbances

THE FIRE IN
THE BIRDBATH

and Other Disturbances

by William Allen

W. W. Norton & Company

NEW YORK/LONDON

Published simultaneously in Canada by Penguin Books Canada Ltd.,
2801 John Street, Markham, Ontario L3R 1B4.
Printed in the United States of America.
The text of this book is composed in Palatino.
Composition and manufacturing by the
Maple-Vail Book Manufacturing Group.
First Edition

Library of Congress Cataloging in Publication Data
Allen, William, 1940–
The fire in the birdbath and other disturbances.
I. Title.
PS3551.L437F5   1986   814'.54   85–10556

ISBN 0-393-92249-8

W. W. Norton & Company, Inc.
500 Fifth Avenue, New York, N. Y. 10110
W. W. Norton & Company Ltd.
37 Great Russell Street, London WC1B 3NU

1 2 3 4 5 6 7 8 9 0

ACKNOWLEDGMENTS

Versions of the following essays have appeared in these periodi-
cals, sometimes under different titles. "Toward an Under-
standing of Accidental Knots," *The Atlantic*, March 1981.
"The Branch Office," *Esquire*, October 1984. "Zen and the
Transcendent Art of Mowing Grass," *Dallas Times Herald*
(*Southwest Letter* section), June 13, 1982. "How I Became
Unique," *Columbus Dispatch Sunday Magazine*, December
23, 1973. "How Eddie, Marcia, and I Smuggled Pickled
Frogs to El Salvador and Lived to Tell All," *New York
Times*, January 16, 1972. Copyright © 1972 by The New
York Times Company. Reprinted by permission. "A
Whole Society of Loners and Dreamers," *Saturday Review*,
November 11, 1973. © 1973 *Saturday Review* magazine.
Reprinted by permission. "Among the Lofty Texas Liter-
ati," *Capitol Magazine*, December 11, 1983. "The Last
Strand: Lament of a Balding Man," *Esquire*, October 1982.
"What I Really Think about Pigeons," *Columbus Monthly*,
August 1983.

For Eddie and Norma

My guides to the starry night

Contents

THE FIRE IN
THE BIRDBATH

and Other Disturbances

Prologue: Why Some People Get More Disturbed than Others

As I was walking along a sidewalk one ungodly hot day in Dallas, a penguin came out of nowhere in a low, hunched run and bit me on the hand. You might not know this, but penguins bite more like dogs than birds, and we had a pitched battle going before I tore free of the creature's toothy bill. What disturbed me most about the surprise attack was the potentially savage nature of a penguin when he gets too hot. I believe that other people who are bitten by hot penguins just don't mention it, because somewhere along the way they have learned what to expect from life.

I have a friend who leads a happy, satisfied existence. He attributes his happiness to something he grew up with called "The Seven Steps." It was a large picture, a kind of diagram I guess, of inscribed granite steps telling everything important to look for on life's rocky road. There were a lot of pictures etched on those steps, too—for example, there were a little boy and girl on the first step, a mortarboard cap and wedding bells on the third, then after that a mansion on a hill, and so on. On the last step was a single shriveled crone.

My friend told me that he didn't always like knowing in advance about those seven steps. Every time he found himself one step further along, it was an unnerving reminder of his mortality. Yet, when a given step came, he always knew how to act. Minor inconsistencies such as penguin bites apparently were not real issues since the grisly sweep of life was always staring him in the face.

I'm not blaming my family, exactly, for not having that picture up in our little home, or some other form of instruction for how things work, but I do think it helps account for why I'm startled or disturbed at times when some other people aren't. For instance, one night there was a fire in my birdbath. The significance was not so much in the event itself, but in what grew out of it. What disturbed me were the knots in the garden hose—six of them—that kept me from putting out the freak inferno.

I wound up writing about that garden hose and its knots—trying, you see, to design some little part of a granite step of life for myself. In so doing I finally understood—at forty-two years of age—why I have been writing all these years. It isn't for recognition and glory, as I had always supposed, but rather to manufacture some order and meaning for myself. Beyond that, I realized that there is satisfaction in this search for order to be had by other humans on the planet earth, too, whether it's done through writing or playing billiards. The reason is this: when we look for order in chaos we definitely feel less nervous and alarmed and disturbed. Just the act of looking itself seems to help take the edge off.

So, I'm glad to say, my friend's "Seven Steps" turns out not to be the last word. It prepared him for his mid-life crisis all right, but he had to spend all those years dreading it, too.

When I turned forty-two, I wasn't prepared at all, but I hadn't lost any sleep over it, either. When it struck, it was sort of like something that happened to a complacent cat I know and like. His paw was caught in a fold in one of those garage doors with an automatic opener, and he was carried dangling up out of sight into the roof of the garage. He survived, somehow, and learned his lesson: he never goes close to that garage door, no matter how many Glad Bags full of garbage wait within.

I may spend years trying to make sense out of what it means to have reached life's turning point. This book is an effort to do that, and just the activity of it has carried me nicely up one more step on life's rocky road. Meanwhile, I have the satisfaction of knowing one thing for certain: I'll never for one second get my paw close to forty-two again.

Toward an Understanding of Accidental Knots

One night a few weeks ago my birdbath caught on fire, and when I ran with what I thought was a neatly coiled hose to put out the blaze, I was yanked up hopelessly short. I looked back and the hose had six knots in it. All those knots appearing just like that seemed impossible, to say nothing of unjust, and it set off something in me that had been brewing for a long time. It made me decide that I was going to unravel forever the mystery surrounding what amounts to half a lifetime of accidental knots.

As a child I thought that any knots in my life must somehow be my fault. Back then I also noticed that knots I wanted tied often wouldn't stay tied—or they turned into knots totally unsuited to my purpose. Later, though I stopped taking the blame for knots, I still hadn't learned how they worked, the way I was sure other people had. Every time I found a knot where I didn't think there should be one, it troubled me. My phone cord has always been in a snarl—I'm used to that—but when it knotted around the stem of my empty wineglass during the night, I needed to know why. Before I died, I wanted to know why the once straight cord to the toaster on my kitchen counter became so knotted that it pulled the appliance up under the cupboard where it was useless, and finally one day caused the toaster to blow up.

I had always assumed a knot required that the end of something be free to go through a loop and then get pulled tight. This assumption was based on the way I had tied knots; but if I was correct, my problem with knots shouldn't exist. If you hold kite string at one end and tie it to a kite at the other, those enormous, hopeless clumps should never develop—especially if the carefully tied knots in the tail are always going to fall loose.

If this seems like a minor issue, let me say that almost everyone I have asked about knots agrees that they are mysterious and need to be better understood. These people also say that my initial conception of a knot ought to be right.

Now, I'm sure that somewhere, in some obscure treatise on some remote library shelf, the answer lies waiting. Sailors and mountain climbers and window washers—or anyone else who depends on the control of knots—certainly must know more than the average person. The cowboys who continually fool with their ropes in movies and rodeos must do so with understanding and purpose. Rope designers and rope makers must know almost everything about knots. But the information has never reached me—and apparently never reached a good many other people as well. What I am about to tell you, then, I have learned on my own.

First, I bought ten feet of common manila rope,

tossed it on the middle of the floor, and just watched it for a while. It didn't move, which didn't surprise me, so I left it there overnight.

Next morning I realized that, even though the rope hadn't moved, it looked tangled. I picked up the tangle and, sure enough, it didn't snake out into my ten-foot length of straight manila rope, the way it should have. It came up in a clump. I tried to shake loose the clump, then pulled on the ends to free it, but this only made it worse. What I had was a tightly tangled mess that required considerable effort to undo.

The rope hadn't been tangled when I bought it, or before I tossed it to the floor, but somehow the *act of tossing* had caused it to converge on itself. It had happened right in front of me, but I hadn't observed it until the next day—which made me aware that, so far, I was bringing an untrained eye to my task.

It became clear that the act of moving the rope in the slightest way tended to cause it to knot. But why? I inspected it more closely. It consisted of three smaller pieces of rope tightly twisted around each other, all with little clinging hemp burrs sticking out of them. Each of the three pieces was made of long, single strands of hemp twisted around each other. When I took it apart, it wanted to kink back up—as if the rope depended on knottiness to exist.

I noticed that if I tossed the rope in the air, freeing it from the force of gravity for a moment, the rope's inherent forces came into play. All the twisting that had gone into the making of the rope had created internal dynamics which made it seek to converge on itself, to continue to twine around itself—most obviously in the form of loops. And a few loops could form a support for yet more rope to gather and wrap around itself. Any collective movement of the rope—any pulling, for instance—made the loops smaller and the tangles tighter. Eventually all this movement was likely to result in a real knot. The bend of a loop, if tight enough, could constitute that free end I originally felt necessary to the creation of a knot.

So now I postulated: *Given the opportunity, a length of something with an end or a substitute end will, in general, tangle rather than stay straight.*

But this only formulated the mystery, it didn't solve it. I recently ordered a martini with a twist and noticed that the lemon peel was unusually long, looking like a little yellow snake in my gin. Before the drink was gone, that twist had turned itself into a knot. At this moment, the cord to my desk lamp has a knot in it. (Some people would have plugged it in like that, of course, but I never would.) A couple of years ago I went to great lengths to make sure that the cords running to my new stereo speakers were straight. Now they're snarled and knotted to the point where the little wires inside are broken, causing static when I walk across the living room floor. And then I've got the problem with the vacuum cleaner cord.

When I vacuum the rug, it would be difficult for me consciously to make a knot in the cord, assuming that it was connected to both the wall and the cleaner. I think I would have to pick up my large Eureka upright and put it through an even larger preformed loop in the cord. But lately I have watched the cord as I vacuum. It goes back and forth, twists this way and that, is constantly being turned—creating tension and a tendency to twine around itself. Then—and this was somehow a surprise to me in its obviousness—I *unplug the cord* in order to move from room to room. For long moments, there is a loose end—sometimes jerked and flying through the air if I'm tired or in a hurry—and with the tension on the cord being what it is, a knot sooner or later will occur.

It all makes sense, more or less.

The accidental knotting of my garden hose, however, remains unexplained. I have watched it for some time and can only theorize how a hundred feet of stiff rubber tubing can so easily develop knots. When I discovered those six knots, I thought back and realized that the hose hadn't been moved for over a year, during which time it had, I assumed, been lying in a state of unsnarled rest. The tension from the act of looping those coils the year before, and the tautness resulting from my race to the birdbath, could certainly explain some snarling, but six knots? The unlikelihood of it has caused me to look in other directions.

I live in the country, and quite a few animals come around that hose at night, drinking from a crock I leave there which is filled by a very slow leak at the point where the hose connects to the faucet. Dogs and cats and raccoons and opossums and who knows what else probably touch the hose from time to time, and just a nudge could activate the tension already in the rubber. Also, the weather could have any variety of effects. High winds and driving rains and accumulations of snow could move the hose from its natural inert state. The change in temperature could cause expansion and contraction—in other words, movement—to occur.

The grass and weeds growing under the hose, the erosion of dirt caused by the leaky faucet, the aging process of the rubber . . . all of these things could combine to make a knot or two while I lie in bed asleep.

But six? It's hard to believe. Possibly other forces, difficult to understand but in keeping with the laws of the universe, have contributed—such as the changing gravitational pull of the moon, or maybe a preceding configuration of the larger planets. But the laws themselves are snarled. We are told both that the universe is expanding and that the natural tendency of all matter is to converge, to pull in upon itself. I have read—and this is disputed—that our solar system originally formed from condensing hydrogen plasma which pulled in on itself and hardened into chunks that became planets and moons that are now locked into orbits about our sun, which is constantly trying to tug them into its fiery gases.

I've always assumed, as Newton did, that these matters had to do with gravity, but cosmologists say they have to do with something called "degree of curvature," and that the quintessence of curvature—don't ask me how—results in the mysterious black holes. Some say that the universe is in the shape of a saddle, except that it has a fourth dimension which perhaps keeps us from being able to see its tendency toward clumping. Other theorists see the universe as having the shape of a figure eight—which we all know is just a yank away from a tangle or a snarl. Whether the universe is going to tie itself into a knot is still in dispute. The argument has to do with the need for a free end, which the universe supposedly doesn't have, but I personally think it might have a tightly bent loop somewhere, which could amount to the same thing.

Some or perhaps all of the forces in the universe may have contributed to the six knots that defeated me the night I ran to put out the fire in the birdbath.

I just don't know. The problem is baffling. Despite all my research—or perhaps because of it—the number of knots in that length of rubber hose makes me want to consider the possibility that they occurred not by accident at all but by design.

The Branch Office

During my first few months in the country I lost six cats in hideous country ways—though every one them made it back under the house to die. Finally I took my problem to the Cat Woman of Cedar Hill, who has twenty or thirty healthy cats at any given time and more always on the way. I asked how she keeps her animals alive in such a savage environment. "You've been going to the city for your cats," she said and handed over a black-and-white kitten named Scooter with markings that looked like a pair of short shorts. "This is a country cat. Take her home and see how she does." I wondered how this little creature could stand up any better against a rabid raccoon, a blind rattler that doesn't rattle, or the marauding albino wolf dog who comes at night, but I agreed to find out.

When I was first planning to move to the country, I had told everybody that it would be rugged and tough to get used to at first, but I think I really envisioned a sylvan setting where skunks didn't squirt and all the rabbits were tame.

The idea of nature actually being *dangerous* didn't occur to me, but little things, like the sudden loss of six cats, soon had me alerted. I began to keep my eyes open. When something puzzled or alarmed me, I began to inspect it or ask around or even go to the library if I had to. I did anything it took to understand what was going on around me and how to act the next time it happened.

But the more I learned, the more my caution gave way to real curiosity. When I wasn't feeling threatened by such phenomena as lightning striking the same place twice, I actually began trying to figure out how the world works. Though my methodology continued to be primitive, I became a budding naturalist.

As any country person knows, there is wisdom in observing your animals, and Scooter quickly became one of my teachers. Soon after I got her, I spent weeks clearing out an overgrown jungle on the northeast corner of the property—eight acres of wooded, rolling Texas terrain. I put cushioned lawn furniture and a hammock down there and called it my branch office, and I was serious about working in this retreat. But right away there were distractions.

I looked up one sultry afternoon in June and saw that the weather was getting funny. In the city I never saw weather: it was there, of course, but obscured. Now there was weather everywhere. The sky turned a sort of yellow-green, and there seemed to be a growing absence of something, as if there were a leak somewhere and all the air was getting out. Then a great thunderhead abruptly formed, and it started getting dark. I'm not a fool, and I was gathering my things when directly over my head little black tails came wiggling out of the clouds. I sprinted for the house, and when I got there the phone was ringing. It was my wife, a city cat who had gone to Dallas to shop for the afternoon. "Get down!" she screamed. "You're in a tornado!" I grabbed a little TV and a bottle of Scotch and went to a large, stone-encased closet on a lower level of the house. When I got there, Scooter was waiting.

That tornado, which apparently everybody knew about before I did, actually touched down just east of where I huddled, tore the tin roof off a barn, and for some reason tipped over four mobile homes that weren't even very close to the funnel. It was tornado awareness week in the media after that, and I heard all about solar energy rising to a peak in midafternoon and boiling the air into great masses; then these great masses of different temperatures collide and cause thunderstorms, which sometimes generate tornadoes.

I wanted to know the scientific explanation for tornadoes, of course, but I didn't especially want to be told that I had just bought eight acres in a place that people were calling Tornado Alley. I knew that was a term for the whole central United States from North Dakota to Texas, but it was alarming to learn that our town had a little alley of its own. All of Cedar Hill, I found out, was once demolished by a tornado that came through like an elephant eating hay. My neighbor Sid, who is younger than me but who was ancient at birth, and who is also one of the last persons to use the word *Gad*, said anciently, "There was nothing left. Everybody still alive was just sitting on their foundations." He then started telling how the Great Dallas Twister of '57 started almost directly over my branch office, but he saw my expression and eased off a little:

"It's really not all that bad around here. Nothing like Wichita Falls, anyway. They've been hit *four times* since 1958. Gad!"

During the Great Ice Storm of '79 I felt like I was living on one of the moons of Saturn, and if I had stepped outside the house *just once*, I would have skittered right down to the branch office and careened on over into the deep arroyo beyond, where I may or may not have been found after the thaw.

During the Great Drought of '80 I couldn't bear going out back. Most of that time I stood guard over the house with my garden hose, ready to ward off any of the two hundred fires that broke out around us that summer.

I was out of town when the six-and-a-half-inch hailstones hit in '81, which is probably why I'm alive today. Sid said that the white bowling balls came out of nowhere at over a hundred miles an hour, were piled up to two feet deep in the branch office, and, even though it was May, took three days to melt.

From all these things I learned the importance of staying close to shelter—though in this case I have trouble following my own advice. From the branch office it is a 150-yard uphill run to the house. Like a space voyager leaving earth to explore the parameters of the known universe, I need to be away from the house to learn anything about nature. Yet if I get too far away, it will interfere with my ability to survive. So I've settled on at least trying to keep a clear, straight line open to safety, even though this has its obvious limitations.

It's not easy, for instance, to outrun lightning. Twice a bolt zapped the same tree less than a hundred feet from where I usually sit. As a budding naturalist, I have learned that lightning *always* hits the same place twice—assuming, of course, that the place survives the first strike. Lightning took away half my tree the first time and the other half the second. My whole approach to studying nature is based on the assumption that understanding makes us feel better, but it didn't make me feel better when I learned that lightning strikes the earth about one hundred times every second and kills about 150 people in the United States every year; that the average lightning bolt is four inches wide, which seems about right, but that these bolts can stretch across the sky for forty miles, and just one of them generates six times as much energy as the output of all the power stations in the country put together.

I think of myself as living in the country, but the truth is that tract homes are at the front gate now that the economy has picked up. There's a new four-lane freeway a couple of miles from us, and a string of fast-food places three miles long is an easy ten minutes away. But on the property itself, we are just about as close to being in the country as I know how to get. The animals seem to think it's as close to the country as they can get, too, because our eight acres have become a wildlife refuge for rabbits, raccoons, foxes, skunks, opossums, armadillos, coyotes passing through, and (it is rumored) a lynx. We also have copperheads, rattlesnakes, horned toads, black widow spiders, tarantulas, ticks that smell with their legs, fire ants, queen termites as big as Idaho potatoes, mosquitoes hovering like Jabberwocks, and great digger wasps that can think.

If I watch my own animals, I also watch every other

creature that comes around too. We put out scraps at night, then shiver inside, awed by the pitched battles, the savage snorting, screeching, and hissing that starts up right after our lights go off. The scraps were a friendly gesture at first, nothing we necessarily intended to keep up; but now they're expected of us. The animals come and wait for them, and if we don't produce, they eventually start calling. I sometimes go down to the branch office armed with a flashlight and see eerie eyes shining back in different colors, but mostly in shades of red.

Of all the creatures I've encountered so far, nothing scares me like a snake. I'm not phobic about them, but snakes have enabled me to understand a little about how phobic people feel about things. One problem with snakes is that you almost never see them until they're close enough to get you. Once my little John Deere mowing tractor hit a weed-obscured rocky hole in the branch office, and a sound like a thousand locusts came out of that hole. The large rear wheel spun free, and in the hole were rattlesnakes like spaghetti in a colander. I went in high gear for the house, terrified that snakes were all over my tractor, and called the police, which in Cedar Hill isn't all that strange because they have an animal control man who'll come by and, for instance, crawl under your house after a dead cat. Two came this time, in a hurry; but they returned from the hole snakeless. They didn't say I was lying, exactly, but the next week when we called because of another rattler on the front porch, the man took forever to come, and then he came alone. The snake was still there, though, and he carried it off alive on the end of a mechanical snake stick. I called later to find out what had happened, and the fellow said he was having a belt made.

The branch office is also frequented by long bow-legged lizards and by even uglier primitives locally called horned frogs, which are really lizards too. They have the charming ability to shoot blood as straight as a broomstraw out of their eyes if you get them cornered. According to the people in the nearby town of Hillsboro, these little monsters can be sealed in the cornerstone of a courthouse without bread or water and taken out alive twenty years later.

It is primitive creatures like these that intrigue me the most. The dumber and more loathsome an animal looks, the more I feel I'm seeing back toward the Beginning, and if there's anything I want to understand almost as much as how to survive, it's how we ever got started at all.

For that, I look to the bugs. There's usually a lot of peculiar bug activity going on—things like a hundred spiders with pea-sized bodies and threadlike legs four inches long, all doing something up and down together that I think was an orgy. But I've seen nothing to compare with when, out of the corner of my eye, I caught what seemed to be a huge tarantula on its way to the arroyo. I quickly drew my Nike Daybreaks up in the chair and, sitting perfectly still, took the opportunity to inspect.

Right away I saw that the tarantula was terribly involved with something else, something that was blue with reddish wings, about four inches long, and much more lethal in shape than, say, a butterfly. I assumed that the tarantula had itself a nice lunch, but I couldn't have been more wrong. In fact, the other creature, which turned out to be a great digger wasp, had the tarantula, not for its own lunch but for many lunches, for a baby wasp about to be born. I would have thought that a tarantula could take a wasp any day, but that wasn't the case here. In fact, the spider wasn't even moving and was being diligently dragged along by the wasp. I wasn't so afraid now—a grave misjudgment—so I got up and followed the duo for about ten feet, which seemed a long way for them to be going, and finally I got a stick and separated them.

The wasp didn't react the way you might think it would. It didn't fly off or make wild sweeps through the air. It stopped and looked up at me. We had a standoff for a bit, then the wasp went back to the tarantula. But it had been so arrogant with me that I couldn't resist stopping it again with my stick. This time it did become airborne and rose to my eye level, where it hovered. I swung at it and missed but came close enough, and it flew off this time. I went to my chair and then after about ten minutes, on impulse, I looked back around at where the spider was, and sure enough, the wasp had come back. But now the tarantula had *returned to life*, and there was a real struggle going on. The wasp finally won, apparently, because the spider stopped moving, but then instead of dragging the spider along, the wasp flew around my chair and hovered again in front of my face.

I wasn't prepared. I didn't have my stick. I wasn't at the proper angle to spring up before it could get me, so I just sat there, pressed back against my cushion, and silently begged it to let me alone. Ten seconds later, seeming satisfied that we understood each other, the wasp returned to the tarantula. I watched them from my chair until they disappeared into the woods.

Later, I learned how digger wasps select a certain

species and size of tarantula, paralyze it, and put it in a large hole they dig for their wasp larvae. They lay several eggs and attach each one to the abdomen of a different spider. When the little wasps hatch, they grow up eating their own personal paralyzed spiders alive. But the striking thing is that this particular type of wasp seems to have actual intelligence, and even though the tarantula *can* kill the wasp, the spider is operating on mere instinct, which in effect allows the superior, thinking wasp to lead it around by the nose. I *thought* that digger wasp was thinking when it came around and began to menace me, and sure enough, it was.

What Scooter did at night was a mystery, though I just assumed she hunted field and barn mice a bit to keep her paw in, and stayed clear of the skunks and killer raccoons. Then late one night I heard my dog Sunny barking from her dog run. This was a first for Sunny, since she usually dives in her little house right after dinner and then drags out of it for breakfast the next morning, so I got up and went out to see what was going on.

Sunny, it turned out, was calling to Scooter, who, on that night at least, was sitting in the open field. It seemed odd, though I don't know why it should have, for the cat just to be sitting alone out in the dark in the middle of nowhere. I let Sunny out of her pen and we walked on over to where Scooter was. On the way I saw a falling star, and just as we reached her I saw another one. Then I realized that Scooter was watching the sky.

In a few minutes another star fell, and I decided something puzzling or even alarming was going on, so I got a lawn chair and Sunny and I joined the cat. We sat out there that night for over three hours and saw by rough count over 150 meteors fall, including something that possibly only Scooter, Sunny, and I, of all the creatures of the earth, witnessed. A tremendous green fireball, straight out of that old movie *It Came from Outer Space,* started falling at the zenith and was still going when it disappeared behind the tree line. I didn't hear it hit, but there in the sky just over the trees a faint little puff of smoke drifted by.

At about two in the morning I realized just how clearly I was seeing the stars. The Milky Way was an absolute river of light going almost from one end of the sky to the other. Because of air and light pollution in the city, I had only really seen stars like this before on Cub Scout camping trips and army bivouacs. But I'd always had a keen interest in the *idea* of astronomy anyway, and now that I was actually living where there were stars and meteor showers, I was moved to invest in a telescope and take up observing as a hobby.

This new telescope of mine was no toy. It was a real scientific instrument, and the day it arrived in its shiny green packing trunk was a glorious occasion for me. Assembling such a complex precision instrument was so intimidating that I actually read the directions, and it still took forever, but I finally got it done.

It took so long, though, that my friends and neighbors were clamoring to look through it, and I made the mistake of inviting them over on my first night of observing. A dozen people sat around in lawn chairs and on blankets for well over an hour while I tried to find something for them to see. First I had to align the telescope's polar axis with the polestar, no small matter; then I set about trying to line up my right ascension and declination coordinates on such deep-space objects as the Ring nebula in Lyra, the globular star cluster in Hercules, and the Horseshoe nebula in Sagittarius. But I saw nothing.

The conversation hummed behind me as I practically stood on my head, twisting this way and that in ways no left-handed person should have to do and think about numbers at the same time. As the pressure grew, my precision flagged and I became more and more confused. I tried to block out all the talk, but I still remember Sid trying to field questions from my city friends. When there was a cry off in the woods, somebody said, "Sid, what was that?" "That was a screech owl," he said. "What do they do?" somebody asked. "That's about it," Sid said. "They're just little bitty things. Gad."

I never found anything that night, and finally all the beer and popcorn were gone and everybody left. I realized later, though, that I really had seen almost everything I had searched for, but the objects were such faint, pinhead-sized smudges that I didn't relate them to the beautiful, enlarged, color-enhanced pictures in the telescope's brochure.

I observed alone after that, and I did come to sort of enjoy looking at those tiny smudges. I know that to look into deep space is to look back in time, and I'm told that it will be the astronomers who will finally understand the Beginning. So I keep looking, for the idea of it if nothing else. My wife observes with me out of pity sometimes, but always winds up saying, "I'll stay out if you just won't make me look at anything else." I always agree, and all sprayed down and sitting in her lawn chair with a glass of wine, she can usually endure at least another hour.

We did have one thrill together looking through the telescope. From her chair my wife called my attention to a great shimmering web, at least ten feet in diameter, being constructed between two trees by a huge garden spider. The moonlight on the web created a spectacular effect, and on a whim I trained the telescope on the nucleus of the web, to which the spider kept returning as part of his method. Magnifying that spider eighty-one times made it so large and gave it such detail that we could see hundreds of filaments being pulled out of the spinneret in his abdomen as he dragged himself forward, and his hind legs worked vigorously to bring all these tiny strands together into one silk thread that to us looked like a rope. I understand that during the Silurian period (over four hundred million years ago) there were scorpionlike creatures as big as gorillas, and that's just about how big this one looked. It looked otherworldly, too, and its web seemed grander than any galaxy.

When the Cat Woman was next over for coffee, she told me how meteorites used to be worshiped by primitives as gifts from heaven—and that, in fact, there's still a nice black one being worshiped by pilgrims who go to the holy city of Mecca. Apparently scientists don't fully understand what I've heard characterized as uninteresting space debris. For instance, it's a recorded fact that meteors like to fall into the maw of newly formed volcanoes, yet no one can explain the attraction.

I noticed the Cat Woman peering into her cup and asked if something was wrong. She said, "Just a little dust from Mount Saint Helens." I think she was kidding, but at any rate the remark got me to thinking about cataclysmic upheaval and, dreadful though it is, how much more socially acceptable it seems than, say, typhus or mass murder or even war. Why do such catastrophes—volcanoes, earthquakes—always seem so remote? The truth is, of course, that they aren't. In one way or another there has been or will be cataclysmic unheaval right in our own backyard. That fact was driven home the day the cannonball, fired just over one hundred years ago, emerged into my space-time continuum, as lethal as ever, not more than fifty feet from my cushioned lawn chair.

Actually, Sunny spotted the cannonball first and was uneasily sniffing it over, as if it might still be smoking, which is what drew my attention to it. The ball appeared as a rusty lump in the branch office, just to the right of the path I've worn by coming and going. I have to mow and trim and prune and hack around there continually to keep back the jungle, so I knew that it couldn't have been there all along and just overlooked, and I wondered if somebody was pulling something on me.

The first thing I did was get Sid, my ballistics expert, over to confirm that this was indeed a cannonball and not just a big ball bearing off one of the first locomotives to chug through Cedar Hill a century ago. He confirmed it, all right. It was a ten-pound shot, six inches in diameter. Who fired it we're not sure, since there is no record of a fight involving cannons ever going on in this area. But a gang of Civil War veterans from both sides did get together here to form a company to fight in the Spanish-American War, which they never got to do; maybe they fired off a cannon shot or two anyway, just out of excitement.

Later the Cat Woman was able to tell me how the

ball got to where it is today. It had, she said, been forced up out of the ground from a combination of erosion and the shrinking and swelling of the soil during dry and rainy periods. And her theory has been borne out since then, because I've had to pick up at least a dozen big rocks that have appeared like Easter eggs in the branch office in just the same way.

It turns out that Cedar Hill is on the extreme northern edge of the Balcones Fault, running up from around San Antonio, and that fault accounts for the fact that we're on hilly ground, three hundred feet higher than nearby Dallas, which is as flat as a pool table. Sixty-five million years ago most of Texas was a shallow sea full of monsters almost fifty feet long; one, an elasmosaur, looked for all the world like that famous blurred picture of the Loch Ness monster. Overhead sailed flying reptiles with fifty-foot wingspans. Then there was enormous earthquake and volcanic activity to the south, and the dust from the volcanoes settled here in layers up to two feet thick in the water, killing the tiny creatures we now walk on and call rock.

That cannonball fired over one hundred years through time, and missing me by fifty feet, made me realize that my gradual awakening to nature had just begun. I began to see complexity and contradiction all around me.

For example, put a digger wasp in a cage overnight with a tarantula, and in the morning it will be the digger wasp who is dead and devoured. *Try* to make a horned frog squirt blood from its eyes, and see how far you get. And for all we know about tornadoes, no one can explain how, twenty-four hours after Cedar Hill was wiped out, a pitchfork fell out of a clear blue sky and stuck up in the middle of town. Also, tell me what caused abrupt one-hundred-mile-per-hour winds over at Whitney to raise the air temperature instantly from 70 to 140 degrees. Or explain why so many blackbirds recently dropped dead in a nearby parking lot that they had to be swept up with industrial brooms and cremated in a Dumpster.

Now my imagination, if I let it, can make the air in the branch office turn black with ash and poisonous vapors. I can envision sea monsters, more than a hundred times bigger than anything I've ever seen, rearing up in the arroyo and swallowing Scooter whole.

When we begin to deal with all physical forces through all time, nothing is simple. All things become possible. All magic and superstition and claims of pseudoscience are dwarfed by the mysteries contained in just my four-dimensional chunk of space iron. For instance, there is a concept having to do with energy accretion that makes it possible, in theory, for the single flap of a seagull's wing to change the weather of the earth. And if all that could happen just from the flutter of a few feathers, what awesome forces could the cannonball have put in motion that will possibly alter just about everything everywhere forever?

Zen and the
Transcendent Art of
Mowing Grass

As a youth, I hated to mow so much that one day I left our push mower in the yard to rust and became an expatriated Texas writer. My first story was about an alien being who, in the end, turned out to be a lawn mower.

By the time I came home again, I had spent so much time in the East that my Texas friends expected me to move into a high-rise in downtown Dallas. But instead we settled sixteen miles to the south, in Cedar Hill. We surprised everyone by buying a place with an eight-acre yard.

It was during the summer, and I had to start mowing immediately. "You just stay inside where it's cool," I told my wife, who is afraid of grass. "I'll take care of the yard." As I spoke, I was gazing out at more grass and weeds than I'd ever seen in my life, except at a cemetery.

Now whenever anybody from Dallas comes out to see our spread for the first time, they remark on the seclusion, the spaciousness, the scenic beauty. Then they ask uneasily, "Do you *mow* all this?" People don't like it when I say yes. They don't understand it. Old friends say I've changed, implying for the worst.

But there is a difference between what I do today and the mowing of my youth. Mowing a little patch of front yard is typical outdoor city work: boring, undistinguished, pitiable, drone-like activity. But getting astride a John Deere tractor and spending twenty hours in two days tackling tough thistles, high Johnson grass, giant sticker weeds, and creeper so tough it copulates with barbed wire is the kind of intense activity that, if you survive it, eventually transcends itself. Like Zen or long-distance running, it becomes a path to wisdom.

I've been at it three years now, and it's no accident that I don't write as I used to. All I really want to write about is mowing—and then for only an hour or so at a time between whole days on my tractor. The fact is, mowing and writing fill the same needs, only mowing does it better.

Mowing eight acres every week would drive some kinds of people mad, but it has served to make me feel in harmony with the flux of the heaving earth as it hurtles through time. I have learned the patience of Job, I don't care if I go bald anymore, I sleep like a baby, and my penmanship has improved.

When I first got on our little John Deere 110 mowing tractor, I thought I was getting away with something. Because I was sitting down and riding, it didn't feel like work—yet it created the perfect illusion of work. I would get nicely sweaty and dirty, and the sound of the tractor chewing up fallen limbs frightened my wife. All that and the long hours I logged convinced her that I was working inhumanly hard. My only concern was that she would try it herself and see how easy it was. Meanwhile, for the first time in my life, I achieved a uniform tan.

Then the tractor started breaking down. The engine blew up from lack of oil. The battery went dead from lack of water. One belt broke, and this inspired all the others to break. I got flats from the spike-like thorns strategically placed by their mother trees for that purpose. I left a trail of nuts and bolts and much larger chunks of tractor that I couldn't identify.

The jungle was taking over, and I had no choice but to call in seventy-year-old Bill Chapman, who arrived on his giant John Deere looking like General Patton. In just three hours he sculpted our steep, rocky, briar- and weed-covered terrain into a work of art. Then he sat down under a shade tree and fixed my tractor. Since that time, he has become my mowing mentor, and I can only wonder at what he knows after almost a whole lifetime of mowing.

He taught me that you don't have to be mechanically inclined to fix a tractor. It's a matter of attitude. A tractor knows if you're afraid of it, or if you have weak resolve. When I leave town and my wife timidly climbs on the machine, it always breaks down—just as my dog quickly becomes rude and unruly in my absence. Once a tractor knows its master is willing to spend all eternity to fix it, then it will run and only break down enough to keep its dignity.

Though a tractor is a crude, man-made, hopelessly earthbound device, its function of mowing conversely sets us on the road to nirvana. Mowing goes beyond the reach of human language, but I would say that it's something like a bright, green dream dominated by sound. The sound is a deafening roar which on given days may contain any number of other sounds, such as clatters or squeaks. There are no people in the dream, which creates a feeling like a martini, and the urge to mow forever is so strong that when you stop, there is a disconcerting sense of moving backwards.

But to balance this dream world, real things are continually happening. For instance, our hills are steep enough in places to turn the tractor over. Or, since one of the tractor parts that fell off was the brake, I could always fall in reverse over the eastern ridgeline, snap through the fence, and careen into the arroyo below. And there are new cavernous animal holes hidden in the weeds to watch out for, as well as snakes, tarantulas, fire ants, and great digger wasps of high intelligence.

Besides the spiritual advantages of mowing, I sense that to mow is to possess. Legal ownership doesn't seem to enter into it. My place didn't feel like mine until I was able to mow it. And the natural urge to expand is always there, of course. Yet, at my youthful age and on a little 110, I would never dare to head out the front gate and try to take over Cedar Hill.

But I have seen Bill Chapman mowing over twenty miles south of here, hunched forward atop his great machine, staring straight ahead, his face the color of a tan that has gone all the way through and come out the other side.

Philosophers have long told us that focusing our efforts allows us to achieve otherwise impossible heights. And so it occurs to me that a man with enough mowing hours under his belt could perhaps levitate or walk through walls. And if a man could mow far enough, he could actually possess the earth, or at least all the way to Pampa, Texas.

Bridey Murphy
at the Dairy Queen

My wife believes in all sorts of things, except perhaps subatomic particles and DNA, and I humor her
in her superstition, for there was a time when I
believed in such things as reincarnation myself. In my
youth, I was bolder than most in my dreams of a more
exotic world than the one in front of my face.

It began, I believe, right at puberty, when I first
read *Frankenstein* and *Dracula*. From ages twelve to
fifteen, when I first literally had the power to create
life, I instead involved myself in fantasies of necro-
mancy; life from life was too easy—life from death
was the challenge. For a while, it was a pitiful one-
boy revolution against mortality, but by the time I
turned fifteen in the middle 1950s, I had two allies.
Eddie was a biologist. Charlie was an electronics wiz-
ard.

I was a mere science fiction writer, but I had something else to contribute to our common cause of
achieving life after death. I was the only boy in our
tenth-grade class to own a car. A car is not just a sym-

bol of power—it *is* power, and it's freedom. My 1953 Ford with shaved hood and deck, skirts, and Oldsmobile taillights broadened our horizons in many ways, but mainly it gave us the chance to go fast.

We needed speed and danger and to be outside the law in order to live close to our nemesis Death. We needed to know him, to embrace him in this early stage of necrophilia, if we ever hoped to emerge on the Other Side in one piece. We wanted immortality as much as our heroes Conan Doyle and Houdini, and were willing to take almost any risk for it.

Except we weren't fools. We wanted proof, too, and when we were sixteen we found it. We discovered *The Search for Bridey Murphy*, a book about a woman who under hypnosis was age-regressed so well that she sailed right on back to before her birth. Her hypnotist found himself talking to an Irish girl, Bridey Murphy, who turned out to have been the patient in a prior lifetime.

I read the book again and again, stunned. It was utterly convincing. The hypnotist certainly seemed credible. And the proof was wonderful. Bridey Murphy herself spoke *on tape* of past events that were absolutely accurate, but that *the patient could not possibly have known.*

Bridey Murphy set us free. If it didn't give us direction, exactly, it made us not afraid to look; the key, of course, was that once you believe you will never die, the conviction radically affects the way you live.

Among other things, our new knowledge meant that there was far more to existence than met the eye. All things became possible, even probable. For instance, ESP should be easy next to reincarnation, and we actively began testing ourselves with the famous five-symbol deck of parapsychology cards that Dr. Rhine had devised at Duke University. We decided that, once out of high school, we probably would give up all and go live at the Edgar Cayce Association for Research and Enlightenment in Virginia, where we would hone our psychic skills and use them for world good.

Before now, without proof, we hadn't had the courage for such convictions. There had been the distinct possibility that there really was nothing more to life than what met the eye—that, try as we would, the mundane lives of our poor parents would be our fates as well.

But the ultimate freedom and source of exhilaration for us was that, if we chose, we could trade in this vale of tears any time we damn well pleased. The willingness to die—since there *was* no death in the ultimate sense—made us overnight superteens of the fifties. Now we were impervious. Now we could drive at breakneck speeds and not *worry* about it.

It's a glorious thing to have conviction, especially in a matter such as immortality. Our present reality took on a bittersweet quality that made us want to stay around. Now that there was escape, there was no hurry to leave the prison. Instead, we could do things to help out here on earth, take up physics, say, and hurry up man's conquest of space.

In short, we had found the consummate religion: one that was not contingent on faith.

Meanwhile, at school we were viewed as outcasts, rebels, and—if our grades were any indication—fools doomed to failure. Nevertheless, we were unnerving to our teachers who could not say, for sure, that we were stupid. Though school itself was beneath us, we were eager to learn, and through some now-forgotten word of mouth this craving caused us one night to wind up sitting at school desks in the back room of a neighborhood Dairy Queen.

All we knew was that the two new and enigmatic managers of the Dairy Queen apparently were authorities on hypnotism and were giving a lecture on the subject. Even as they walked into the room, I remember feeling in awe of them; I sensed that any word they uttered would have more value than a year of study at the Tower of Babel called South Oak Cliff High. They were both in their twenties, I think. One fellow was ordinary-looking in a pleasant sort of way. He was someone I could identify with. But the other seemed from another planet, which of course was perfectly possible in our current scheme of things. He was thin, and his teeth were bucked. He had a three-inch-long bristly crewcut, if you can imagine that, and wore thick goggle-like glasses. The overall effect was that of a young Jerry Lewis playing the role of a mad scientist.

They had studied in Europe, they told us, and after a brief history of hypnotism and the scientific principles involved they asked if there were any questions so far. "What about age regression?" I asked.

The Man from Mars, as I already fondly thought of him, smiled. It was a smile suggesting not only knowledge along those lines, but also a consuming secret interest. "In due course," he said.

Then he proceeded to hypnotize everybody in the room.

In my memory, it seems as if there were about ten of us there, in ages ranging from sixteen down to, I fear, eight or so. I don't know just how successful the

Man from Mars was with the mass hypnosis, but after we all had ostensibly been put under, he perused our slumped little ducktailed heads to select the best subject for further work.

I was the best, and though I don't know how he determined that, I know I felt proud, like I would have at scoring highest on an IQ test or being best at guessing Dr. Rhine's ESP cards. The Man from Mars had me come to the front of the class and sit at a desk away from the group. There he proceeded to take me to the Seventh Level.

It is a distant world, the Seventh Level, and I know that if you have never been there I cannot recapture it in a way you will understand. It felt mystical, all right, and peculiar, like just before you pass out on an operating table. But once I had gotten there, the Man from Mars made what I considered a terrible misjudgment. He said that I now had the ability to see things that weren't there. For example, he said that I could visualize a motion picture cartoon on the wall. Then he asked me to go ahead and see that cartoon.

I certainly wanted to see it, and I tried with all my heart. I even thought I *could* see it, a little bit, but I wasn't absolutely sure, so I finally said in a trance-like tone, "What kind of cartoon?"

After a moment, he said, "A Donald Duck cartoon. Isn't it funny? Don't you want to laugh?"

I got the message, but apparently the Man from Mars hadn't heard that laughter or even smiles didn't come unearned from a superteen of the fifties. (This is borne out by snapshots of me from that period. I wasn't as gloomy a teenager as I looked, but I wasn't in a state of hilarity all the time either.)

Then I thought I got a glimpse of, strangely, Porky Pig, and I managed to laugh weakly at the idea of seeing a pig when I was supposed to see a duck. The audience shrieked in delight and, even on the Seventh Level, I felt like a fool.

The Dairy Queen was soon closed down, then later reopened under new management. Who were those guys? Were they frauds? Embezzlers? Con artists? Or in some way full of evil design? We never found out.

Bridey Murphy itself was soon under fire. An entire book was written debunking it; though evil design was not ascribed, it simply had not held up when tested by the scientific method.

Thus began the cynicism in my nature that friends remark on more and more with each passing decade. I had come to understand the brutal and exacting concept of *fallacy*. During our last year in high school, we lapsed into decadence and made bombs. We never hurt anybody with them, and though we tried to blow up a bridge once, it didn't budge; like all our crackpot schemes, the bridge bombing was sound without fury. We used my car to take girls to the Dairy Queen— and we parked out front where we belonged.

But it was not entirely lost on us that through all of our romanticism, superstition, and decadence, we had had a need for our convictions to be substantiated. In fact, I would like to propose another crackpot theory: that we were among the first generation ever to be born with inductive reasoning in its genes.

Now I'm a man who for the most part has pitched his fate with *hypothesis*, *experimentation* complete with *controls*, with plenty of *repetition* and always a wary eye out for *sampling error*. But while the scientific method is an exacting master, hard but fair, it can do nothing about individual backsliding. It is a mystery why a perfectly trained twelve-year-old dog or a forty-two-year-old man will one day stray, but it happens.

Not long ago, I saw a psychic on television. He was being interviewed on the news for having found more missing persons—dead bodies, for the most part—than any other psychic since the Swede Peter Hurkos. On television, this bearded psychic looked like the lycanthropes of my youth, and there were other things about him that engaged me as well. He was a Dallas boy, like myself, and was my age. He seemed like a very nice person, too: sincere, unaffected, modest, yet nobody's fool, either.

A few days later, I read about him in the newspaper. A sheriff in Louisiana was calling him over to look for somebody thought to be dead in a swamp. Just a week after that, I saw him interviewed on *That's Incredible!*

My wife was impressed with him—and she knows her psychics. I can't explain it, exactly, but something snapped. All my cynicism went away. Here was a fellow doing something that, it seemed to me, couldn't be faked, at least not again and again. If a gang of police, after exhaustive searching, can't find a body, and then this person has a vision and points to a map, and the body is where he pointed, then it seems to me that it proves once and for all that psychic ability exists. The hell with sampling error and controls; this guy got results.

My youthful zeal had returned. If I believed in the fellow, then there was nothing to do but go after dead bodies with him. I would write a book about him and, scientific method or not, the world would know at last that ESP is real.

I called him up. I went to his home, in the suburbs of North Dallas. He looked even more like a wolf in person than on television, except now I could see that he was a quite overweight wolf. He said he had always been large—and had, in fact, once wanted to play professional football. As a teenager, he had been a ham radio operator; he had been poor in English, good in math; he had liked girls. He had been normal in every way until one day he was struck by lightning and became psychic. My wife, who was with me, afterward reconfirmed that he was the genuine article.

Once he and I got to know one another better, he confided: "I really hope you can write something about me. I need the publicity. Being a psychic is a tough way to make a living. I'm always under pressure to find another body. Still, if I can find just two more, I'll have it made. I'll be ahead of Hurkos. I can get on *That's Incredible!* for an unprecedented third time. I can write my own ticket."

We talked about his methods, and he was disarmingly honest. "It's ninety percent common sense. I'm really a pretty decent detective. All good detectives are psychic, anyway. Mainly, I get a feeling about the missing person—whether he's dead or alive—then if he's dead I'll get an image of the location of the body. After that it's hard work—a lot of looking, more thorough than what's been done before. Usually the body's just been overlooked. I come in with new energy, a fresh eye, and eventually we might find it. Of course, I bomb out a lot, too. Most of the time, in fact."

After my last visit, on my way out, his wife came home loaded down with groceries, and she said that she was a psychic, too. His mother was as well, I had learned. She performed at parties. My man said he did too, as well as give private readings. He gave me some pamphlets as I left—touching, amateurish little things with horseshoes and four-leaf clovers on them. They were called "How to Improve Your Luck."

I truly believe in this psychic sleuth. I'm convinced that, for once, I have come on a truth without testing. But where is the romance? I think that with a little common sense and hard work, I could be a psychic myself. My wife is probably good enough right now to do parties. A book about the guy just wouldn't go over; it wouldn't be glamorous enough—especially up against such wonders of modern science as black holes, the electrochemical mysteries of the human brain, the knotted rings of Saturn, and the golden toad of Costa Rica.

It's a hard lesson for the boy I once was. (And for the boy I may be again if I'm right in my fear that I'm entering second childhood.) But the fact is that all the things we have found to be true through science are more wonderful than anything we will ever dream up to believe in. Except, of course, that nothing can ever be quite so wonderful as the dreams themselves.

How I
Became Unique

All my life, I've wanted to be unique. Even as a small child, I always felt that I *was* unique—that one boy who stands apart from all the rest. Perhaps it was because I came from a broken home, was an only child, parted my hair on the wrong side of my head, was left-handed and dyslexic, put my belt in backwards. I don't know.

It is ironic and fitting that when I really did become unique it was in a physical sort of way, because as a child I was never a good group player during recess. It is an example of how we Americans overcome ourselves, make strength out of weakness. We do it through sheer *desire*, fostered by *proper attitude*, and may my own success inspire all you throngs out there who are tired of being nobodies.

I became unique by setting a world record. Back before *The Guinness Book of World Records* was even very popular in this country, I was a great fan and relished each new edition. I liked knowing and being able to tell others that the world's chug-a-lug champ consumed 2.58 pints of beer in ten seconds, that the world's lightest adult person weighed only thirteen pounds, that the largest vocabulary for a talking bird was 531 words, spoken by a brown-beaked budgerigar named Sparky. There is, of course, only a fine line between admiration and envy, and for a while I had been secretly desiring to be in that book myself—to astonish others just as I had been astonished. But it seemed hopeless. How could a nervous college sophomore, an anonymous bookworm, perform any of those wonderful feats? The open-throat technique necessary for chug-a-lugging was incomprehensible to my trachea—and I thought my head alone must weigh close to thirteen pounds.

One day I realized what was wrong. Why should I want to *break* a record at all? Why not blaze a trail of my own? Now, as you can see, I definitely had desire, but more than that I discovered I had talent. My gift— broom-balancing—was developed in my back yard when I was a child. When I remembered the unusual ability, I immediately wrote the editors of the Guinness book in London.

Dear Sirs:

I have read with enjoyment *The Guinness Book of World Records* and want you to know that I intend to contribute to your next edition. Thinking back today, I recalled that as a child I had an uncanny talent for balancing a common house broom on the end of my forefinger. Rushing to the kitchen, I found that I have retained this gift over the years. Since almost everyone must have at some time attempted this feat, I think it would be an appropriate addition to your book.

I would like to know exactly what must be done to establish a world record—how many witnesses, what sort of timing device, etc. If you will provide me with this information, I will provide you with a broom-balancing record that should astonish your readers and last for years to come.

Sincerely,
William Allen

The reply came the next week.

Dear Mr. Allen:

In order to establish a world record of broom-balancing, we would like to have the confirmation of a newspaper report and an affidavit from one or more witnesses. With regard to the timing device, I think that a good wrist watch with a second hand would prove sufficient for this purpose.

Please let us know the duration of your best effort.

Sincerely,
Andrew Thomas
Assistant Editor

It sounds simple, but a lot of preparation must go into setting a world record. You can't just set it. You must advertise, generate public interest. The purpose of this is to lure in the news media. It's absolutely necessary to have a write-up if a record is going to stick. And, of course, one wants the article for his scrapbook later on. Imagine what would happen if you just went into the bathroom and brushed your teeth for eight hours and then called the newspapers. They would think you were crazy. But if you generated interest beforehand—involved a local drugstore chain, got a name-brand toothpaste to sponsor you— then you wouldn't be crazy at all. You might even come to be something of an authority and make a career out of promoting things to do with teeth.

I took a slightly different tack. I ran an ad in the college newspaper which read, in part: "FREE BEER! FREE BEER! Come one, come all, to Bill Allen's Broom-Balancing Beer Bust! Yes, friends, Bill will attempt to balance a common house broom on his forefinger for at least one hour to establish a world record. The editors of *The Guinness Book of World Records* in London are anxiously awaiting the outcome. The evening will be covered by the press. Come one, come all to this historic event!"

May I suggest in general that anyone trying to set a record find himself a good manager. My roommate, Charlie, was mine and he proved to be invaluable. On the big night, he drew with chalk a small circle on the living room floor so I would have a place to stand. He cunningly scattered copies of the Guinness book on the coffee table. He had the good sense to make me wear a coat and tie: "You don't want to go down in history looking like a bum, do you? Of course not. You want to make a good impression."

The ad in the paper paid off, naturally. Over fifty people showed up, filling our apartment and spilling out onto the lawn. Some left after their two-beer limit, but most remained to see the outcome. There was some problem, though, in holding the group's interest. For the first ten minutes or so, they were fine, placing bets, commenting on my technique. After that, their minds tended to stray. They began to talk of other matters. One couple had the nerve to ask if they could put music on and dance in the kitchen.

Charlie handled the situation like a professional. He began to narrate the event, serving as a combination sportscaster and master of ceremonies. "Ladies and gentlemen, give me your attention please. We are at mark fifteen minutes. At this time, I would like you to look at Bill's feet. You will notice that they are not moving. This is an indication of his skill. If you've ever tried broom-balancing yourself, you know that the tendency is to run around the room in an effort to maintain stability."

Someone said, "He's right. I tried it today and that's exactly what you do."

At the twenty-minute mark, Charlie said, "Ladies and gentlemen, I have an announcement. Bill's previous top practice time was twenty minutes. He has just beaten his own record! Anything can happen from here on in, folks. Pay attention."

You might be wondering about my emotions at this point. I hadn't slept well the night before, and all day I had been a nervous wreck. I hadn't been able to eat. I had a horrible sinking feeling every time I thought about what was coming up. But once I started, I found I wasn't nervous at all. Not a trace of stage fright. In fact, I blossomed under the attention. I realized this was where I had belonged all along—in the center. Someone began to strum a guitar and I foolishly began to bob my broom in time to the music. "Don't get cocky," my manager warned. "You've got a long way to go yet."

At mark thirty minutes, Charlie held up his hands for silence. "Listen to this, folks! The halfway point has been passed! We're halfway to history! And I want you people to know that Bill is feeling good! He's not even sweating! I swear I don't understand how he does it. How many people can even stand in one place that long?"

I had no clear idea who was in the room, or what

they were doing. In order to balance a broom, you have to stare right at the straw. I'm not sure why this is, but it's certainly the case. You can't look away for even a second. By using peripheral vision, I was able to see a vague sea of heads but it wasn't worth the effort and I gave up. While in this awkward position, I heard the low, sinister voice of a stranger address me: "You know everybody here thinks you're crazy, don't you? I think I'll just step on your feet and see how you like that. You couldn't do anything about it. You wouldn't even know who did it because you can't look down."

"Charlie!" I called. "Come here!"

My manager had the situation under control in seconds. After he had hustled the character out the door, he said, "Don't worry, folks. Just a heckler. One in every crowd, I guess."

I must say that Charlie's earlier remark that I was in good shape was a lie—and I was feeling worse by the second. At mark forty-five minutes, my neck seemed to have become locked in its upward arch. My legs were trembling and the smaller toes on each foot were without feeling. My forefinger felt like it was supporting a length of lead pipe. But more startling, I think, was the strain on my mind. I felt giddy. Strange that I have this gift, I reflected. I can't even walk around the block without occasionally wobbling off to one side. It suddenly seemed as though all the balance normally spread throughout the human body had somehow converged in my forefinger. Wouldn't it be ironic, I thought dizzily, if I just toppled over? I sniggered, seeing myself flat on my back with the broom still perfectly poised on my finger. Then I began to observe the broomstraw in incredible detail. Each stick seemed huge. They looked like trees.

"Are you okay?" Charlie asked. I snapped out of it and reported my condition. He turned to the crowd. "Folks! With only ten minutes to go, I would like us to reflect on the enormous physical and mental strain Bill is suffering right before our eyes. It's the price all champions pay, of course, when they go the distance, when they stretch the fibers of their being to the breaking point." His voice became lower, gruffer. "You may as well know, Bill has been hallucinating for some time now. But think of it, folks. While all over this country of ours people are destroying their minds with dangerous drugs, Bill here is achieving the ends they seek—" his voice rose; he cried, "—with *no chance* of dangerous after-effects!"

Even in my condition, I knew he was going too far. I called him over to loosen my shoelaces and whispered, "Cut the speeches, okay? Just let them watch for a while."

The hour mark came amazingly fast after that. There was a loud ten-second countdown, then the press's flashbulbs and strobes began going off like starbursts. Everybody began clapping and cheering. Using my peripheral vision, I saw that the crowd was on its feet, jumping around. I saw the happy, grinning faces.

I kept balancing. Charlie conferred with me, then yelled, "Folks! Bill is not going to stop! He says he will balance till he drops! Isn't he something? Take your seats, ladies and gentlemen. You're witnessing history tonight. Relax and enjoy it." The group was for seeing me drop, all right, but they didn't want to wait around all night for it. They became louder and harder to handle. They wanted more beer. At mark one hour, fifteen minutes, I was on the verge of collapse anyway, so I gave in and tossed the broom in the air. With a feeble flourish, I caught it with the other hand and the record was set.

But no world record is *truly* set until someone has tried and failed to break it. After the congratulations, the interviews, the signing up of witnesses, it was time for everybody else to try. They didn't have a chance, of course. Most lasted only a pitiful few seconds, and the two best times were seven and ten minutes. These two had talent but lacked the rest of the magic combination.

My record never appeared in *The Guinness Book of World Records*. I got a letter turning me down from a McWhirter brother himself. It was a strange letter, asking me to set the record again, this time with a tray and glass of water on top of the broom. I was indignant. I refused, pointing out how it would mar the purity of the act. It wasn't until years later that I began to wonder if there was a cloaked message in the conditions the man stipulated. Sometimes I am haunted with the idea that I didn't go long enough, that it would have taken something more like twenty-four hours to put me over the top.

But the wonderful thing is that none of that mattered. The record had been set, whether it was in the book or not. I had the write-up, and that alone brought me all the acclaim I could handle. To this day, the record has not been broken, either, and I'm still a party favorite because of it.

There is a man in Iowa who collects dirty oil rags. He has over a thousand so far—more than anyone else in the world. He's not in the Guinness book, either, but people will stop by almost daily to see his collection and ask his opinion about this or that. His picture often appears in the local papers.

That fellow's success story is, in a way, more pro-
found than mine, because he made it big without
unusual ability. When I heard about him, I realized
that I could have set the world's record for wearing a
nickel taped to my forehead. For carrying a brick
around the longest. Or for fitting the most pennies in
my mouth. Given my ambition I would have suc-
ceeded no matter what, because I have what it takes
to be unique. Talent helps, all right, but in the end
what matters is still old-fashioned desire fostered by
proper attitude.

How Eddie, Marcia, and I Smuggled Pickled Frogs to El Salvador and Lived to Tell All

June 2, 1971
Board Greyhound for San Juan, Tex., with $200 cash and Master Charge card. In dubious standing with Master Charge. Leaving university life for good. G.I. Bill exhausted. Professional student days over. No prospects for future in land of opportunity. Victim of the times. Thirty years old and can't find work. Outstanding credentials worthless. Seven years college. Hard worker and honest. Type 60 words per minute, no errors. Leaving country for fresh start in El Salvador, Central America.

El Salvador is land of volcanoes. Land of eternal spring. Going down with long-lost high school friend, Eddie, and his wife, Marcia. Wrote him last week after poring over yearbook. Told him of hopeless situation. He wrote back he was leaving for new position at University of El Salvador. Said to rendezvous at San Juan on Tex-Mex border, try Central America for change of pace.

Seems Eddie sprinted ahead in last 10 years. Ph.D.

Biologist. Ecologist. Writer of articles, books. Knows frogs inside out. Discovered frog never before known to man; named it after wife. After reading letter I rushed to atlas, was amazed at remoteness of country and tiny size. Sixty miles wide, 160 long. Two thousand miles from Texas border through Mexico and Guatemala. Pass bus trip to San Juan writing farewell post cards and reading paperback, *Ten Keys to Guatemala*. After many stiff and grimy hours arrive in Rio Grande Valley. Dust-covered shrubs stretch to horizon. English ceases to be predominant language of fellow travelers. Pitch and timbre rise. Babies less disciplined.

June 3
Joyous reunion with Eddie and Marcia. Sit up into late-night hours whooping over high school days. Marcia has retained 79-pound mosquito-like countenance but Eddie huge after lean early years. Stomach evidence of remarkable success in life. Make plans for trip which is to take one to two weeks in Land-Rover, depending on side excursions. They've been before and there's much consulting of maps, consideration of alternate routes. Pretend to be absorbed but too ignorant of geography to contribute much. Cover by using words like "isthmus" and "meridian" and calling Pan American Highway "Artery of the Americas."

June 4
Pull out of San Juan early in Land-Rover. Reynosa border crossing only minutes away when Eddie mentions Mexican officials might want to cut my hair. Feel indignant. Hair perfectly acceptable in most civilized

locales and I wonder if this is bad omen. Eddie should never have mentioned it as fears turn out to be unfounded. Pass customs without a hitch. Some problems with Land-Rover since it is loaded down with sealed boxes, suitcases, jars of pickled frogs, a lunar globe, and "The Recorded Works of Beethoven." Customs inspector wants to know what's what, threatens to make us unload, but Eddie gives him a dollar and we're waved on through. "I wasn't worried about Mexico," he says. "It's Guatemala I dread. We'll have to unload everything there. I'm sure of it." We're a hundred yards into Mexico when a cop begins waving and blowing his whistle at us. Eddie panics, lurches through red light. Cop runs up and for some reason begins talking to me.

Talking to me in Spanish like talking to a stone. Only one year in ninth grade. Can count one through six and say: *¿Cómo está usted? Muy bien, gracias. ¿Y tu? No comprendo. El Presidente está en la Casa Blanca.* Eddie says the cop is asking if I'll do the driving during our stay in Mexico. I lamely admit my license expired in 1969. Eddie gives the cop a dollar and we drive on. Ten in the morning and already incredibly hot. Am keenly interested in everything, particularly burros and cactus. At noon I drive Land-Rover for first time. Keep arm out window to hurry along tan. Drenched with sweat, love it. Feel the winter melting away. Swig warm Pepsis and think of T. E. Lawrence.

June 5
Second day south of the border and already deathly ill. Stayed overnight in Victoria at $4 hotel and insisted on eating everything Eddie warned against. Soaked whole meal with evil-looking green sauce. Was cocky

because have never been subject to stomach problems. Eddie and Marcia fine this morning but I was up most of night and head now bobbing like sick chicken. Notice for first time Land-Rover is truly miserable vehicle. Hard to steer, awkward to shift, bounces all over road, won't go over 50 miles per hour without heating up. Respect for British shaken. "It's not much on the highway," Eddie admits. "But we'll need it where we're going. It's the only thing besides a donkey that'll get up most of the volcanoes." "We're going up on volcanoes?" I ask. "Sure," he says. "That's where I'll be catching my frogs."

Hour later while passing through small town we're caught in flash flood and Land-Rover stalls on cross street. VWs, Chevys, everything else, pass us by. "It's still got a few bugs in it," Eddie mutters as he grinds starter. Water recedes, Land-Rover starts, desert soon behind us, weather cool after rain, vegetation lush and varied.

Some type of tree with bright red-orange flowers dominates countryside. Marcia very impressed with this particular tree, insists on pointing out each one individually over a 20-mile stretch. Grass and mud huts line road. Women mostly seem to be beating clothes on rocks or wandering around with something or other balanced on heads. Men mostly sitting on stoops or wandering around on burros. Little boys get to run naked but little girls have to wear clothes. Come to a sign: TROPICO DE CANCER. Insist on having picture taken next to it for literary friends. Begin to feel remote from civilized world. Begin to keep eye open for dread fer-de-lance, a brown and yellow snake whose venom can kill in minutes. Antidote available but we don't have it.

Four days and 800 miles into interior. Left tourist crowd back at Mexico City and now cresting Sierra Madre del Sur. New respect for Cortez. Mountains Kool-Aid orange and green. Incredible craggy vistas along endless inclines and snaky curves. See what looks to be a seer perched cross-legged on a rock. Lizard-like skin and waist-length white hair. Three-foot beard parted into pigtails.

Am thrilled. Want to get out and say, "Tell me, old man, what the years have taught you." Don't know how in Spanish. Serious mistake not to have tried harder in ninth grade but will make up for it. Will attack Grosset's *Spanish Phrase Book and Dictionary for Travelers*. Will learn 10 phrases, 20 words each day. Have sudden urge to give up English altogether, master Spanish and start life over in El Salvador. Be great Spanish novelist. Have vision of living in mud hut with buzzards on top, grand-looking roosters strutting in and out, skinny pigs fooling around outside. Could be another B. Traven. Could write another *Treasure of the Sierra Madre*. Would send out manuscripts by native courier on donkey.

June 7
Cross Isthmus of Tehuantepec and see both Atlantic and Pacific in same afternoon. Prefer Atlantic. Whitecapped emerald water with sand-dune beaches. Hire sullen boatman to take us in leaky motorboat up remote river overhung with gnarled-looking trees on stilt-like roots. Would be fitting to see brontosaurs crane necks over tops of trees, pterodactyls roosting in upper reaches. Boatman seems to steer deliberately into low-hanging vines, moss, and spider webs big as fish nets. Spider silk getting in hair, eyes, mouth.

When I turn and glare he looks away, scowling and muttering under his breath.

Finally come to cul-de-sac where boatman cuts engine and demands payment for ride. Occurs to us he might try to dump us when he gets money so we say half now, half upon safe return to Land-Rover. He agrees. On way back Eddie says parrots, monkeys, and alligators are in this area but all I see are the huge spiders whose webs are turning us into cocoons. Spiders strangely clean-looking and hairless. Bodies like pink eggs with piano-wire legs.

June 8

Arrive in Tapachula, last Mexican city before entering Guatemala. Head directly for Guatemalan embassy in downtown Tapachula to have visa stamped in passports. City large and crowded but streets the size of most alleys. Police on boxes at intersections blowing whistles. Impossible to tell what they want. Spotted one blowing whistle when no cars around. Catchy little tune like bird in springtime.

Locate embassy and sit dumb with fear as Eddie and official get into loud argument over my passport. Can't understand a word but sense official has edge because he speaks higher and faster as argument progresses. Shakes his head, points at me and shrills, *"Imposible! Imposible!"* I hunch forward trying to look earnest, innocent, and deeply concerned (all of which I am but don't think it's coming across). Then Eddie spots some up until now unnoticed squiggle on passport and begins speaking higher and faster. Official's eyes dart uncertainly and for a moment his voice drops. But then he rises half out of chair, talking louder than ever and triumphantly jabbing squiggle. Eddie slumps back in seat, sighing, "*Si, Si.*" Can't stand it any longer and blurt something about trying to make it back to U.S. alone. Eddie looks bemused, then realizes I have no idea what's going on. "It's nothing like that. You've just got to pay $2 for a tourist card."

After we leave he explains that though my passport appears expired, it's actually good for two more years because U.S. passports were recently extended. I know this. I also know that foreign countries were notified of the extension. What I didn't know is some countries like Guatemala pretend not to have gotten the news, apparently to collect tourist card fee.

We get into Land-Rover. Beautiful girls along narrow street throw kisses, wave, and beckon with open arms. I thumb through phrase book for "Let's go get a beer together," but can't find it. Happen onto "I love you." *Te quiero. Te amo.* Start to yell that but realize how stupid it would sound. Sit mutely as Eddie drives on. Develop theory that sexual incompetence directly proportionate to verbal incompetence. Register at high-class resort hotel, sit in plush bar and gaze out picture window at distant Guatemalan mountain range. Have learned how to order beer efficiently. *Una cerveza por favor. Tiene usted* Carta Blanca? If place doesn't have Carta Blanca I turn it over to Eddie to get me whatever they've got. Then when I want another I hold up bottle and say, "*Señorita! Una mas por favor.*" Figured it out myself. Eddie says it's not the best way to say it but admits it works.

June 9
First introduction to Guatemala is border guards waving guns at us. Soldiers all look like bantam-weight boxers. Stone faces. Wear straw cowboy hats

with brim pinned up, sleeveless shirts, and ammo belts criss-crossed over chest. Never so aware of Mexican hospitality till now. Endless paying of fees (including something called Extraordinary Service Fee because we arrived after 11 A.M. and before 2 P.M.). Waiting more unpleasant because of grim prospect of having to unload at any moment.

At least I'm spared all haggling because of ignorance of language. Am able to wait in Land-Rover with Marcia. Eddie must bear all. Hear him get into shrill arguments at every turn. Marcia explains if they make mistake on our papers here we suffer when we try to leave country. For instance, if they copy motor number wrong guards at other border might claim it's not same Land-Rover. Last time they were here an official got not only motor number but license and color of Land-Rover wrong. Also misspelled Eddie's name.

At one point Eddie comes over quickly for conference. Says there's guy who can get us through without unloading if we slip him $20. Marcia says that's too much. I suggest he tell crook to shove it. Eddie goes back but soon returns with look of wonder and relief. Says that's it, we can go, that evidently they're not going to search us after all. "They didn't even mention it after I told that guy to shove it," Eddie crows.

We drive on, gleeful we didn't pay the exploiter any money, then a storm cloud suddenly tumbles over a nearby mountain and is on us in seconds. "I might have to stop," Eddie says. "I can't even see the hood." I put my face against the glass. "I can see a little," I say. "There's a building ahead and more guards. They're waving at us to do something. Can't tell what. Wait a minute. They're saying pull into the building.

Looks like some kind of garage." Eddie finally maneuvers Land-Rover inside building, confers with soldier, then turns to us, pale. "This is where we have to unload."

Under way after three nightmarish hours unloading every box, unpacking every box, repacking every box, reloading every box. Eddie's dread justified. Soldiers found nothing suspicious except electric razor; at first they thought it to be radio transmitter en route to guerrillas. My opinion of Guatemalans dropping steadily. Finding out things Eddie was hesitant to tell before now. Grisly stories of tourists murdered by guerrillas for cars. Land-Rovers in particular demand. Daily assassinations of government officials. American ambassador assassinated here, only one ever lost in whole world. Should have read up more on subject before leaving States. *Ten Keys to Guatemala* woefully inadequate. Observe everyone is armed at least with machete. Eddie suggests that most Guatemalans live in dense jungle and must cut way in and out every day. Marcia wryly remarks on astonishing rate of plant growth.

Skinniest dogs in world here in Guatemala. Must drive around them as they have lost will to live and won't get out of road. I mention to Eddie we haven't seen a single cat. "That's understandable," he says. "They were probably consumed years ago." He wants to take two-day sidetrip into mountains to see Mayan ruins but I refuse. Uneasy about being gunned down. Never worried about that before and don't bear up well under it. Urge we go most direct route to El Salvador. Stop for nothing but gas. Eddie says okay but it will mean driving at night when guerrillas are out.

June 10
Wound up staying overnight at motor hotel in
Esquintla, Guatemala, to avoid possible guerrilla
ambush. New day and feel more magnanimous toward
country. Slight setback when waiter at hotel restaurant can't understand my order. Think he is being
difficult like the French, but Eddie explains Guatemalans aren't used to American accents like Mexi-
cans.

Under way again and beneath blue sky Guatemala
seems most beautiful, exotic place on earth. Towering
palms and coconut trees rising out of lush rain forest
full of long-legged white birds. Backdrop of sweeping
mountain range with clouds snagged on peaks. Have
impression people are more friendly today. Begin to
see Indians in multicolored costumes. Eddie still
complaining about missing Mayan ruins and I am on
verge of giving in until he notices story in newspaper.

"You remember those people running by the hotel
last night and all those sirens?" he asks. "Well it says
here the guerrillas gunned down some government
official right down the street from us. Wait a minute.
It was an official's brother." On to El Salvador. Ask
Eddie if Salvadorians are peaceful. "Oh, sure. Most
peaceful people on earth. The only thing they'll fight
over is athletics." "Athletics?" I ask. "Yeah," he says.
"They got into a little war once with Honduras over
a soccer game." Fantasy of country forming in mind.
Paradise on earth. Happy land full of childlike, sports-
minded people.

June 13
Truly the land of eternal spring. Weather in El Salvador like California coastline above Santa Barbara. Truly

the land of volcanoes. Seventeen in country the size of New Hampshire. Only here three days, yet have already decided never to leave. Border crossing example of happy, athletic nature of people. Had to unload there, too, but soldiers helped and didn't wave guns. Played like children with Eddie's stuff. Tossed his lunar globe back and forth and chased each other with pickled frogs. Eddie irked but I think world needs more of this playing around.

Already settled in upper-middle-class section of town on lower slope of Volcán Boquerón. Whole city of San Salvador, population 300,000, built at base of this dormant volcano. Wonder about term "dormant" as Boquerón still heats water for our neighborhood. Last erupted in 1917 and Eddie says it's sure to blow again. Question is, of course, when. Comforting illusion of permanence created by radio and TV station antennas on top and giant sign in lights on side hawking local loan company.

Each afternoon around five, rain clouds boil over crater giving us eternal spring showers. Already into habit of having drinks and watching clouds instead of five o'clock news. House is three-bedroom Califor-nia-type stucco with maid quarters. Marcia wants maid so she can lie in bed and eat chocolates all day. Labor cheap. Maids $15–$20 a month. Rent cheap and food reasonable except for American imports. Campbell's soup $1 a can. Can't buy diet Shasta.

June 16

Spending days soaking up sun, hoping one day to pass for native. Eddie made generous offer: indefinite room and board and Spanish lessons in return for help with frog collecting. Will spend free time writing, get

Eddie to translate, become established as Salvadorian writer. Maybe El Salvador's greatest writer. Maybe El Salvador's only writer. Will also sell manuscripts to United States publishers, double money. Soon be able to have own house with nubile maid in every room.

Spending evenings with front door open for cool breeze. Frogs on way to local pond drop in for visit, five or six every night. Eddie keeps jar of formaldehyde by chair and waits till specimens hop within reach. Vampire bat zooms in tonight, sends Marcia screeching out of room holding head. Also friendly neighborhood policeman drops in, says he will give house special protection for $10 a month. Eddie asks why we need special protection. Cop says everybody knows North Americans are rich. Eddie says thanks but no thanks.

June 17
Eddie's duties at university outlined. Will counsel graduate students, study population problem, do definitive work, "Frogs of El Salvador."

June 18
Downtown overcrowded and squalorous. Want to mingle but am held back by language barrier. At six feet am tallest person in town. Find huge marketplace honeycombed with tiny shops. Endless good deals. Stumble onto five-block-long red light district. Women in cages almost. They stay in tiny rooms with bars on front like jail cells. Ordinary housewife-looking types sitting on couches reading magazines. Don't know whether they go off with customers or just pull a curtain. Natives buzz around town in midget cars that make Land-Rover seem like Panzer. Will take taxi next

time. Great deals on movies. Admission 50 cents to 75 cents for most North American films. Women get 5-cent discount.

June 19

Reach top of Volcán Boquerón today after three-hour climb in four-wheel-drive vehicle. Land-Rover truly magnificent. Peer into half-mile-deep crater and am stunned to see huts at bottom. Eddie suggests that in such a small, overcrowded country it's the only place left to get away from it all. One of his Salvadorian colleagues who's with us says, "We're small all right. At one time the United States was spending more on Vietnam in one day than our national budget allows for a year."

Spectacular view of San Salvador below and along horizon is blue line of Pacific. Port Libertad and beach only 30 minutes from city and we plan to go in near future. "Port Libertad is very nice," Eddie's colleague says. "But not as nice since the oil ships started cleaning tanks offshore." When we ask whose oil ships, colleague gazes squint-eyed out to sea and says "Yours." On the way down a group of peasants see our license and hold out hands for money. When we don't give them anything one takes lazy swipe at our tire with his machete. Eddie asks about anti-American sentiment here. Colleague puts two fingers close together. *"Un poco."*

June 21

Must get used to local customs. Had dinner at home of another of Eddie's colleagues and found chicken foot in soup. Almost ran from table but contained myself and located other foot in colleague's bowl.

Watched him and found he didn't actually eat foot, only spooned up soup around it. Soup good despite thoughts of where foot must have walked and scratched during stay on earth. Fleeting notion of trying to sell idea to Campbell's. Campbell's Chicken Foot Soup. A claw in every can.

June 22
Should have given friendly neighborhood policeman $10 a month. Thief broke in while we were at movie, took stereo, TV, two frozen chickens, half-full bottle of Booth's High and Dry, and my typewriter. Dormant Volcán Izalco rumbled on coast today. Once called Lighthouse of the Pacific and soon may be again. Bath water scalding this morning.

June 23
One of Eddie's American colleagues, an embittered botanist from Indiana, came by complaining about incredible import tax the Government wants him to pay on car. Seventeen hundred dollars for 1963 Impala. Said he wasn't going to pay. Said he was trying to work something out. Said Eddie was in same boat with Land-Rover and had better start working something out, too.

June 25
Eddie came home early because of student unrest. Wonder if happy nature of people flagging. Gangs of students going around campus shaving heads. Not certain who victims are but disturbance clearly not over athletics. DOWN WITH YANKEE IMPERIALISM painted on several buildings. Also TAKE THE WAR INTO THE STREETS.

June 26

Government confiscated Land-Rover. Said it had to be inspected to determine value before levying import tax.

June 27

Besieged by giant ants today, fearful creatures who turn and rear when you try to step on them. If exterminator doesn't come by bedtime plan to put bedposts in cans of kerosene.

June 28

Botanist from Indiana came by today with new midget car. Jokingly greeted us with, *"Viva la revolución!"* Said he was planning to sell Impala to avoid paying tax. Expounded virtues. Rebuilt V-8. New whitewalls, new brakes. Radio, heater.

June 30

Import tax only $250 for $4,000 Land-Rover compared to $1,700 for $600 Impala. Strange logic at work here but Eddie of course keeps mouth shut and pays. We start to leave inspection station and find Land-Rover won't start. Notice gas gauge on empty, put in can of gas, drive on, then see gauge falling to empty again. Find hole punched in tank apparently by thief who couldn't find gas cap. On way to have new tank put on when transmission and rear-end fall out. Estimated repairs $900, but parts not available in El Salvador.

July 1

Miss Walter Cronkite.

July 2
Botanist from Indiana returns looking harried. Can't sell Impala because whoever buys it would have to pay $1,700 tax. Only person who could buy it would have to leave country for good in next few days. Asks when I expect to be going home. I say I'm not. Asks if I'm aware of the political situation here. Says I'd be smart to get out while I can.

"The military could try a takeover any day now," he says. "If there's a coup you know where you'll be don't you? Between a machete and a machine gun." "If it's so bad," I ask, "why don't you leave?" He looks distant and martyred and says, "This is where my work is. I have to stick it out." He looks mysterious and slightly crooked. "Anyway there's . . . uh . . . certain problems about my going back to the States just now." He slides his chair closer, hunches forward. "How about if I give you the car for $100? Rebuilt engine, new brakes, new tires . . . you could get $600 for it in the States." Profit motive strong. Offer too good to dismiss lightly but idea of driving back alone makes sweat pop from my upper lip. Sudden vision of breaking down in Guatemala, being fought over by guerrillas and fer-de-lances. "I can't do it," I say, "I'd never make it."

July 3
Botanist from Indiana right. Land of volcanoes in more ways than one. Eddie came home early again today, was told to stay put for duration. Campus in state of anarchy. Military marching on university. Charm of country wearing thin. I suggest we return to States while there's time but Eddie says, "It's not as bad as

it looks. These Central American countries flare up all the time but it never lasts. We'll stick it out.''

July 4
Sticking it out.

July 5
Whole country suddenly on verge of upheaval. President fled to Costa Rica. Coup feared. Eddie insists there won't be a military takeover because of sizable middle class. Expounds on childlike nature of people (fun-loving but quick-tempered).

July 6
Spanish grammar tedious.

July 7
Wake up in middle of night to rattle of machine guns coming from direction of university. Last shred of courage vanishes. Spring from bed, tell Eddie and Marcia they can stay around if they want but I'm getting out first thing in the morning. All hope of contributing to Salvadorian literature gone. Get botanist from Indiana up and make purchase. Odds of making it back to States alone slim. Can't speak the language. Three border crossings. Passport that everybody pretends is expired. No insurance. No driver's license. Also found out Indiana plates on Impala expired. Only thing worse is staying here and being gunned down over drinks.

July 8
Thirty hours on road in low-flying Impala. Far cry from Land-Rover. El Salvador and Guatemala already far

behind. Saved at last minute from clawing way back alone. Eddie and Marcia at side. Was loading car at dawn when they appeared with two suitcases, lunar globe, and jar of frogs. Said they decided to sit out turmoil in safety of States, fly back later. Well into Mexico and won't stop until across Texas border. Dead-tired and having fantasies. Fantasies of blond girls who speak the language. Fantasies of diet Shasta, Lemon-Lime and Wild Raspberry. Fantasies of catching up with news with Walter Cronkite. Fantasies of $500 profit on sale of car. Fantasies of fresh start in land of opportunity.

Flailing Around
a Remote Habitat

Once we had traveled four hours out of San Jose by Jeep up into the Tilaran mountains and checked into our hotel, Eddie put a picture of a toad on the restaurant table and announced his first objective. *"Bufo periglenes,"* he said. "The golden toad."

This toad looked like someone had held it with tweezers by one small toe and dipped it in a bottle of Day-Glo hot-orange paint. It was nothing less than the brightest of all the creatures of the earth, except perhaps for certain of those glowing subterranean fish. It occurred nowhere else on earth, either, except two miles up the road in the Costa Rican cloud forest.

Eddie's guide from San Jose nodded wisely, though I didn't know why, since I had learned that he hadn't even been to the forest before, except once with Eddie almost twenty years before when they had first found the toad together. They plotted on a map for a while, and the decision was made to plunge immediately into the jungle after the toad.

I could have gazed out the window at the green mountains for a while longer, but opted to plunge along with Eddie. I had learned that there were howler monkeys down here, and didn't want to miss any opportunity to get in that forest and see one. I wanted to look that monkey in the eye, to satisfy a long-term curiosity about the almost perversely bellicose beast.

A lot has been said about the impression the virgin Monteverde Cloud Forest Preserve makes on people the first time they see it. I have heard of people having religious experiences upon entering the forest. I have heard of others turning around and running out as if for their lives, though they couldn't say exactly why. You walk up to it as if up to a great vegetative wall, then with one step you're in an environment almost as alien as being under water—which, given the humidity, you almost are. Besides the wetness, you are struck by the darkness beneath the canopy, the stillness, the silence, the fecundity, the great size and density of the trees, the layer upon layer of strange forms of green growth, all strung together by endless tendrils and tangled vines. Though the forest is full of noise-making creatures, they naturally are wary at first, and if you don't stay in one place and be quiet, you may never hear anything except the sound of your own screams as you slither off the steep wet trails.

Our guide led us along a nature trail for tourists in a soundless crouch that Daniel Boone would have envied, tapped with import all the numbered markers which were in plain sight, then confidently took us three miles into the jungle, straight to where he said the toad should have been but wasn't.

Back at the hotel, we sat at the bar, wet, muddy, and tired as the clouds boiled over us and lightning flashed and cracked and hissed right outside the window. I had hardly ordered my drink when Eddie made one of those fast moves I had come to be so wary of since he had once gotten me into a coup in El Salvador. He announced his intention to pack up and leave for the coastal lowlands without delay.

I stared at him. "You mean tonight?"

"Right. We can make it to Limon, get a good night's sleep, and be on the river tomorrow."

His main purpose in coming to Costa Rica, it turned out, had little to do with the golden toad. He had mainly wanted to see it and photograph it again out of herpetological nostalgia.

The grant money paying for the trip actually was to catch another, more common variety of toad which didn't occur in these high altitudes. When pressed, he said he hoped to play the toad's distress calls back to the toad itself, to see what the toad thought about it, if anything. Eddie's plan, then, was to go to far Tortuguero, near Nicaragua on the Mosquito Coast, to a spot virtually unpopulated by humans, full of steamy lowland swamp, crocodiles, vipers, and yellow fever. The guide was eager to take him, too.

Eddie could have gotten me to Tortuguero if we had just gone there first; I wouldn't have known the difference. Or he could even now if he could convince me that I was an essential part of his research. "How do you do it?" I asked.

He shrugged. "Find the toad, turn on the Uher, and see if the toad hits the water."

All things considered, Monteverde seemed sublime by comparison, so I elected to stick around for the next two days and look for howlers.

I contacted a local guide named Barry who met me at the hotel at sunup. This fellow turned out to be an encyclopedia of Costa Rican flora and fauna, which he shared at a dizzying rate over breakfast. I mentioned that I had an interest in howler monkeys, and he said there were several troops in the forest, one of which was rumored to be eighteen strong, led by a dominant male called Old Joe by the local humans.

Neither of us had a vehicle or animal to carry us the two miles up to the forest, so we hiked—too fast, I thought. Barry was in good shape, of course, and wasn't even breathing hard. He talked all the way, pointing out various mosses, lichens, wild orchids, bromeliads, several butterflies with transparent wings, and a great python centipede with fangs.

Once we were deep in the jungle, it turned out that Barry's true passion was the elusive resplendent quetzal. His passion verged on obsession, I thought, and I guess I misled him into thinking I shared his fervor. He said not to worry, that he wouldn't let me leave Monteverde without seeing a resplendent quetzal.

This long-tailed red and emerald bird, which once supplied feathers for the headdress of Aztec kings, has been called the most beautiful bird in the Western world. It occurs only in the wet forest ecosystems, and is so special that elderly birders will make last-ditch pilgrimages to the forests to see one. I wanted to see one too, I guess, but my heart wasn't in it after a while. I was exhausted, for one thing, from the two-mile uphill dash to the forest in that thin air, and the harder Barry tried the more I realized that I actually disliked birds. I had kept various kinds as a child, not out of affinity, but because my parents only allowed me to have *contained* pets, and birds seemed better than, say, tropical fish or crickets in a cage.

Also, what I really wanted to do was sit down and sip water and let nature come to me. The only rest I got was when my guide would stop to listen to the bird's call, a monotonous "woo woo" that seemed miles away, then play his tape recorder with its weak batteries back at the remote noise, hoping to bait the bird with his own call. We never did see a resplendent quetzal—my loss, I know—but he did lead me to a small troop of howler monkeys, though we didn't get very close, and by then we were in a real downpour anyway.

"Great job," I panted. "You showed me a howler. Let's get back to the hotel." He had shown me one, of course, sort of, but more than that he had given me the secret of finding them: Listen for their yell. Determine which way along which ridgeline they're heading. Then charge up the ridge ahead of them at a right angle and be waiting when they troop through the canopy.

The trick for me, I had learned, was to do my investigations on my own, and for five hours that afternoon I slogged around alone with my boots full of water in this eight-thousand-acre sponge. As a weather-sensitive person with aches and pains ready to go at the slightest encouragement, and one who has bad associations with humidity in general, I can't explain why these three days of saturation never once bothered me.

The clouds, which are carried almost continually through the forest by the Atlantic trade winds, can be solid as thick fog or have the phantasmagoric shapes of dreams. The forest muffles sound, and the sounds that are heard are strikingly loud and singular and resonant. Surrounded as I was by things called tree ferns and elephant ears and strangler figs, and with lizards dashing everywhere, the overall effect was otherworldly, and on this second day it brought on a brief attack of cosmic loneliness, a condition which before now I'd only felt in late adolescence. While I wanted to feel a part of everything around me—and I thought I eventually could, as an individual—as a *species* I began to feel like an unworthy brute. I thought I'd like to take that fanatic Thoreau, give him his share of existential *angst,* then tie him to a strangler fig and see if he'd do all that much better. During this low point, I took a picture of myself and had the most dismal, forlorn expression on my face since army bootcamp.

Then a troop of howler monkeys began to call. Before I even thought what I was doing, I came out of my *angst* and took off after those monkeys. It is hard to exaggerate the difficulty of lunging through the dense jungle, especially in the rain and where the jungle is on the side of a mountain. Sensibly, you need a machete to get through there, but of course you can't touch a leaf in that protected forest. When I had chased along after my guide, it had seemed easier. He seemed to know hidden paths. Now, almost before I knew it, I was disoriented and practically tied to the trees by vines and limbs and undergrowth. Everything seemed designed to snag me, but even so I was resolute and focused only on catching up with the monkey sounds.

These monkeys are terribly misnamed. They don't howl at all; they roar like lions, and the sound would be horrifying if you didn't know the creature making them seldom weighs over twenty pounds. I was making a lot of noise myself, as you might imagine, and I hoped this actually would work in my favor. The howler monkey doesn't like to put up with anything and is known to go out of his way to yell in your face. But when I felt sure I was somewhere near them, they fell silent.

Since I didn't know which way to go anyway, I stopped to catch my breath and began to look up in the trees, which in places is impossible because of the thousands of plants growing around and on one another in exotic cooperative ways, but I thought I caught a glimpse of something up there, and sure enough I had.

They appeared, at first, as vague shadowy vegetative growths that moved. There were a few slight cracks in the canopy, giving a backdrop of light, which further blackened their shapes, but I started taking pictures anyway. I should have waited. As soon as my film was gone, the dominant male came forward to size me up, while in the background other younger males followed, and the females, some with babies, huddled back where they seemed to think they belonged.

The leader came down on a lower limb to get a better look, and then made a cautious woof and roar. He began to strut, displaying his golden sidehair and snowy white testicles. I did a woof and roar imitation back, which galled him, and he woofed and roared louder. When he did this, he seemed to become all throat, and held tight to the limb by his great tail, as though he might yell himself loose. I was amazed that the fellow would come so close; in fact he changed limbs again, and was almost directly over me when I realized the inherent danger of being beneath a monkey.

I woofed and roared NO, and he snarled and jumped around like a dog on a chain, though of course he wasn't chained at all and could have pounced on my head in a second. My guide probably could communicate with moss on a rock; I wasn't so advanced, of course, but I definitely felt I had communicated with that monkey.

Once they had moved on along after more leaves and berries, I wasn't lonely anymore, but I was lost. I looked around with that sinking feeling of not knowing one direction from another. I had heard stories of people in blizzards getting lost and being found frozen in their own backyards, and I was just about that turned around, too. But after all, I wasn't in a blizzard, just in a downpour, so before I wandered around and found the main path again, I sat down and ate the cheese sandwich I had carried around in a Baggie all day.

Eddie and his guide were scheduled to return late the next afternoon, and I spent that morning in the hotel restaurant, talking to people associated with an organization called the Tropical Science Center. As I sat looking out over the Nicoya Gulf and listening, it occurred to me that, given my methods, I could have walked around the forest alone for a lifetime and not have learned a thing.

I finally understood the implications of where I was. Southern Central America is a brand-new narrow landbridge (five or six million years old) that connects North and South America, allowing plant and animal species from both continents to converge there. I was perched on the backbone of the little bridge, and on one of my earlier walks had been atop the continental divide, at about six thousand feet.

I had felt like I was on Venus, or my idea of Venus from the erroneous science fiction magazines of my youth, because this landbridge happened to form in the path of trade winds that can bring in two hundred inches of rain a year. Even when it's not raining in the ordinary sense, the condensation from the clouds in the forest causes rain within the canopy. At 3,500 miles south of my little town of Cedar Hill, Texas, which is already over the edge of the earth for a lot of people, there is no winter on Monteverde. It is one of the nicest, most consistent climates anywhere, and growth goes on at an almost record rate.

What these scientists referred to as "life zones" are created by changes in altitude up the steep sides of the Tilarans or even by whichever side of a ridge you happen to be sliding down. There are six zones in the cloud forest, all with names like Tropical Premontane Wet Forest and Tropical Lower Montane Wet Forest, and each evolves its own specialized life forms. The zones are evolutionary islands, creating species which may occur nowhere else.

The species crowd together, are dependent on one another, and cooperate in ways that allow even more growth; the result, in the plant world, is over two thousand species so far discovered and described, and a co-director of the forest preserve guesses there may still be a thousand to go. It seems otherworldly, but it's not; it's the kind of seat of creation we are thought to have evolved from.

Many scientists and ecologists believe that in storehouses of genetic and evolutionary knowledge like Monteverde waits our best chance for curing most human ills—which made this following lesson for the day almost incomprehensible.

Deforestation on a massive world scale began less than thirty years ago, yet in just another fifteen years or so most of the wet forests everywhere will be gone. Just one century later over half the living species on earth today will be extinct. Technology, the human population explosion, hunger, and the attending need for crop and grazing land account for the cutting and burning of these forest habitats.

Costa Rica, with all its national parks and individual efforts by groups such as the Tropical Science Center (which owns the Monteverde Cloud Forest), is one of the few countries doing much of anything about it. I had, by sheer circumstances, become one of the last living creatures to see this aspect of the earth—except perhaps as a kind of great green zoo, which Costa Rica may soon become.

We were talking about how Monteverde conceivably could be a gene bank for restoring future life on earth, when Eddie and his guide arrived, and the conversation quickly changed to toads.

Eddie's guide was vindicated. He had gone to the right place that first day to find the golden toad, after all. Certain seasonal rains the toads like had been a few days early this year, so they had already mated and gone back underground.

But everyone enjoyed talking about this rarest of toads—how it glitters like silent gold coins in the dark forest, coming out by the hundreds briefly to orgy then disappear. These toads seem to have developed their color to attract one another without croaking; they're speechless, and even when a male in his zeal climbs atop another male, the one misperceived can only vibrate his displeasure, a signal for the suitor to get off.

The golden toad is endangered, of course, as are the howler monkey, the resplendent quetzal I didn't see, the three-wattled bellbird, and countless other species of forest life not even yet identified. The more colorful of the creatures are held up as symbols to try to engage people to help save them; but of course it is their habitat that needs saving, and remote habitats just aren't all that engaging to people who, unlike myself, don't magically wind up in one and get to look around.

That evening, at the San Jose airport, Eddie's guide presented me with an autographed copy of a book of short stories he had written. It was a real published book, highly endorsed, with his picture on the back, and I left with the notion that all along he had been doing research on North American scientists like Eddie for his next story.

On the flight home, Eddie had good stories about Tortuguero, how it was virtually untouched by man, one of the last truly savage and wild places on earth. He had sixteen rolls of slides to prove it, too, but he never caught a toad the whole time. All he caught, in fact, was a terrible cold in one of the most temperate climates on earth. The toad work, however, he successfully completed by jetting off to a volcanic region of Southern Veracruz, where he found them in great number.

My pictures of the howler monkeys didn't turn out so well. I can see monkeys in them, but nobody else can, and one Cedar Hill local at Shorty Hood's cafe remarked that he could take better pictures of monkeys without ever leaving town.

Looking Chickens in the Eye

I just returned from Costa Rica, where everywhere I went I saw chickens running proud and free. It was a wonderful sight, taking me back to my Texas childhood when we loved for fluffy chicks to sweep peeping after us like wind across a wheat field.

It was a time when we still liked chickens and they still liked us. We could see ourselves in the chicken. One lacking in courage was said to be a chicken. One given to hysteria was said to run around like a chicken with its head cut off. In Texas at any rate, one with a high-stepping gait was said to walk like a chicken in high oats.

Yet roosters really could be tough and fearless and wouldn't hesitate to flog a person, especially a small person. Game fowls, even while prostrate and mortally wounded, would answer the insulting crow of a victorious rival and make a last effort to avenge themselves before the spark of life departed. Their port and bearing and fiery spirit made them emblems of courage.

Hens clucked and cawed their affection and trustingly dangled their feet as we carried them to the chopping block. An old-fashioned chicken slaughter meant something. For children, it could be unparalleled in horror. To be splattered with blood as it fountained from the headless neck of a thrashing pet made many a callow youth view the universe in a darker light.

Chickens used to be considered grazing creatures and were given range in order for them to lay well. An hour's liberty a day was recommended to keep them happy and in good health. There used to be egg-laying contests, with silver cups awarded to the winners. Proud owners had their pictures taken with the prize birds. Competition was fierce. For example, in the Georgia contest of 1930–31, a white leghorn named Dixiana laid 342 eggs in 365 days, the record in the United States at that time. But her overjoyed owner was defeated that very year by a nameless Alabama Rhode Island Red who won handily with 359 tan-colored eggs.

Man and chicken pitched their fates together so long ago that no one knows exactly when or how it came about, but we do know something about our early relationship. Once domesticated, the chicken was unwilling or unable to show stealth in a wild state. In spite of the common hen's fruitfulness and great maternal virtues, she had one careless habit which alone could have ended the species. Her delight at having laid an egg could not be contained. She had to cackle loudly—and her companions would quickly join in the celebration, announcing any new egg's arrival over long distances. Also, a chicken's habit of roosting before dark and in view of any potential

predator suggests a lack of guile that probably contributed to their fate in modern times.

Today, it's hard to look a chicken in the eye, partly
because that eye has never seen the light of day, much
less the joys of a barnyard. Today's female chicken
lives and dies unseen and unknown, a victim of the
simple process of turning four pounds of feed into
two pounds of chicken in four weeks. After a broiler's
confined, nervous, and generally dismal four-week
life, it is strung up on a conveyor, knocked senseless
with an electric charge, and its throat is unceremon-
iously slit. It is dunked in hot water, plucked by spin-
ning rubber brushes, then decapitated, dismembered,
disemboweled, and packaged. So cost-efficient is the
process that attractively packaging the bird is as
expensive as raising it.

The life of a rooster may be preferable by virtue of
brevity. Most of today's roosters have their fates sealed
on the very day of birth, just as soon as their sex is
determined. A person called a sexer, often an Orien-
tal, sticks his finger into the chicken's anus. If the sexer
finds the chicken to be male, it is simply thrown away
or fed to zoo animals that relish live meals.

The American chicken industry is a paragon of cost-
efficiency. Today's egg factories can house a million
birds each. One of these factories can be the size of
six football fields, filled with cages starting seven feet
off the ground. There are spaces between the cages
to allow skid-steer loaders to remove tons of drop-
pings daily.

Yet the business is still trying to improve, to the
point that more is known about the chicken's nutri-
tional needs than our own. One researcher using
estrogen injections has recently developed a hen that

will lay two eggs a day. The drawback is that the eggs have no shells. They are loosely contained in an unattractive membranal sac. The problem could be overcome with modern packaging techniques, but whether the consumer can be made to eat shell-less eggs has not yet been determined. More hope is placed on a new dwarf hen that eats little but lays normal-sized eggs.

Obviously the American chicken is on its last leg as a creature operating in any semblance of a natural state. Still, it has an amazing resilience and ability to adapt. Probably the best example is its knack for living without a head. Reports of living headless chickens are not uncommon. Typically the phenomenon occurs when chickens have their heads chopped off on a private rather than commercial basis. If the severed head doesn't include a pea-sized part of the brain at the top of the spinal cord, the chicken can live. It can breathe and eat through its neck. It can walk, though unsteadily, flap its wings, and make a gurgling sound thought to be a form of cackle or crow.

Chickens are socially resourceful, too, though circumstances have forced them to behave in ways that may appear aberrant. Near a large metropolitan area some chickens were recently seen living on a grassy knoll adjacent to a freeway off-ramp. No one knows how they came to be there, though it is assumed that they fell from a passing truck. All efforts to capture the entrenched guerrilla-like fowls have been unsuccessful.

In another metropolitan area, whole gangs of American chickens are roaming the streets and living in tenement house hallways. Four-pound chickens have been sighted chasing forty-five-pound street dogs down back alleys.

If I'm right that in a country's chickens we see the country itself, things have come to a terrible pass. We not only aren't doing right by our chickens—we don't even see that we're doing anything wrong, which suggests that we may already be beyond redemption.

A move to Costa Rica may be the thing to do, and believe me I'm considering it. It's a wonderful place where the air is still pure, all the children are beautiful, and the green mountainsides are dotted with farmers raising crops and herding cattle and grazing chickens who will be happy till time for their trip to the chopping block.

You can still count on things in a place like Costa Rica. It's a long but invigorating walk to work. It will rain in the afternoon. And should you ever stop in front of a hut on a mountain road, the chicken of the house will come to the door to give you directions.

The Secret of
My First Book

I know now just how smart I was to have my first book be about the care and feeding of dwarf parrots. At twenty-two, I had only sold two stories to the worst of the men's magazines, and was anxious to stop being filler between pictures of hare-lipped exhibitionists and ads for small-game boomerangs. But my friends, who were literary failures then and still are today, viewed my writing a raise-and-train book as even less worthy than what I had been doing. They asked if I felt guilty about prostituting my art. "A little," I told them, but it wasn't true; deep down I felt sorry for them and their misguided idealism. To get this chance to write a whole book, no matter what about, just seemed like the obvious next step, a way to move my career forward as well as make some real money fast.

Opportunity knocked out of the merest circumstances and might have been passed up by such imperturbable saints as Updike or Cheever. Mailer or Capote might have heard the knock, though, and like them I had ambition and a sense of what sells. To tell

the truth, I wanted to be more than both those pea-
cocks combined: I wanted to be the Elvis Presley of
literature.

It happened twenty years ago in Texas, at a place
called something like the Buenos Aires Bird Ranch.
The term "bird ranch," like the worm ranches of my
youth, was misleading. It really was just another pet
store, admittedly a big one, selling everything from
great Leadbeater's cockatoos to crickets in matchstick
cages. The owner of this store—a man as ordinary-
looking as, say, James Michener—came out of nowhere
and gave me my big break. As I was thumbing through
a thick hardback on ornithology for sale there, he sidled
over and said, "I wrote that book." Then he indicated
an entire shelf of raise-and-train literature and said
grandly, "I wrote all those books."

Texas, at least so far as I knew, was a literary desert
back then, and this was the first real author I had ever
met. To look at him and then look at his picture on
the inside flap of a big published book was eerie and
a little frightening—yet I couldn't have handled myself
better. "What a coincidence," I said. "I'm a writer,
too."

In fact, I handled myself so well that when I left the
bird ranch an hour later, I had a free Halfmoon dwarf
parrot to raise and train. I also had an assignment to
write my first book—a development my wife had
trouble comprehending. She gazed uneasily at the
disgruntled, pop-eyed creature in the cage and said,
"How can that man give you an assignment to write
a book if he's not a publisher?"

It's simple, I told her, and explained the situation:
his publisher's biggest competitor had asked him to
write this book on dwarf parrots. My man wasn't about

to, but he wanted to be nice about it; who could tell, he might need a new publisher someday. So he decided to pass their offer onto another writer—namely me. I finished by adding that they weren't about to say no to me because my man was so big—and, who could tell, they might land him next time.

All that made sense to my wife, but one thing still troubled her. "Why you?" she asked. "He's never seen a word you've written."

With that, I took the bird into my office, along with all the books my man had given me to draw from, and began to set up shop for my new project. I didn't want to tell her I had left the impression that I already knew something about birds. After a moment, I called out: "Maybe he was just in a jam and I came along at the right time!"

The plan was for me to write three chapters and an annotated table of contents to present to the publisher. I would raise the bird for the first-hand personal touch the book needed, then lift any technical information I needed from my man's books. I had hardly begun my research when it occurred to me that, in a way, I was trying to write something about nothing. If you wonder about the term "dwarf" parrot, it may be because such a creature doesn't exist—except in the way that a "pet" cricket exists when you catch one and put it in a cage and sell it to somebody in a store. Of course my little Halfmoon, whom I named Tommy, did exist—but more as a representative of a whole variety of small, parrot-like birds than as a freak of nature.

I quickly found that my bird never existed more convincingly than when he made his many noises, which weren't small or dwarf-like at all. His early-morning cries for food had an especially shrill, demanding quality that my wife grew to hate. The pinfeathered fledgling still had to be fed a special gruel on the end of a toothpick, and he thought of me as his mother. My wife sometimes actually started trembling when my little Tommy got us up in the morning. "You're jealous," I chided, but there was more to it than that. Before this, I had been on the brink of getting a job, and every sound the bird made must have reminded her of my close escape from work.

Still, things went smoothly for a while. I kept Tommy's craw stuffed with gruel, and his feathers became resplendent. The writing progressed so well that I grew cocky. My man knew his stuff, all right, but he couldn't touch me when it came to style. It occurred to me that since I was bringing unusual abilities to this field, I could perhaps elevate the genre. Perhaps I could write the first truly great raise-and-train book, one that would become a cult item for literary types who had advanced beyond the classics. It should be a *friendly* book, I decided, much more fun to read than the flat-out kind of information my man wrote. It would be a perfect balance between instruction and entertainment—in short, a work of art.

When I sent off my chapters and outline, I was quickly yanked back to earth. I got a scrawled note from the publishing company saying that they had no interest in such a book at this time.

No problem, my man told me over the phone. Little snafus like that are the name of the game in publishing. He chuckled as he recalled how an entire edition of one of his books just disappeared between the printer and distributor, then was found months later on a loading dock in California. Another time, right in the middle of a contract dispute, a vital file cabinet in his editor's office just caught on fire and destroyed all record of his association with the company. Still, he said, things do get done. Books get written, published, and even sold. "That's a relief," I said. "So what do I do now?"

"Why don't you meet me at the Y for a steambath?" he said. "We'll talk it over."

The suggestion took me aback, though for different reasons than perhaps it should have. I had never had a steambath. I associated them with fat, bald, middle-aged businessmen in Doris Day movies. Those old guys were all fools and they suffered like hell in that hot steam for all their indulgences. I also was a little afraid of water in general and nervous over the idea of possibly not breathing with perfect ease.

So to get out of taking the steambath, and before I considered what I was doing, I invited this published author, this man of the world, to dinner at our apartment. My wife was furious, and she had good reason. First, she connected steambaths with aberrant sexual behavior, something I hadn't yet heard about. Second, we didn't *have* dinner, exactly; at twenty-two, our idea of dinner was a Chef Boy-ar-Dee pizza with extra pepperoni and a quart bottle of beer. Then, since they were going to meet, I was forced to confess some things. "At least I told him I didn't know as much about ornithology as he did," I said.

"Which means just short of everything," she said. "What you know is to give them seed and water and how to change their papers."

Then I told her something that I had hardly been able to admit to myself. I had committed her to doing the photography for the book. I had told my man that she was a photographer on the side—which in fact she did want to be. "Look at it as your big break, too," I said. She turned to Tommy and studied him with a new eye. "I suppose I could take some pictures of him," she said. "Not just him," I said. "All the varieties. Dozens of them. It's a real opportunity to show what you can do." She grew pale and made her own admission: "I'm afraid of birds," she quavered. "I'm phobic about birds. I always have been."

Of course my man and my wife didn't care for one another, but the evening went better than I expected. In any event, it was blessedly short; after he was served in the living room on a TV tray, he couldn't get out of there fast enough. Then, as I walked out to his car with him, he draped a fatherly arm around me and gave me some glad news. The snafu had been straightened out. The publisher I had written to was out of the country, in Brazil on a trip to do with birds. His wife, a sweet but ignorant lady, had written me with no knowledge that a dwarf parrot book was in the offing. I would hear from him soon, and meanwhile should proceed with the book. With the Half-moon selling season only months away, time was of the essence.

So I forged ahead. "Masa meal is corn treated with lime water then ground," I wrote. "It also contains starch, calcium, niacin, thiamine, iron and riboflavin." After penning those particular lines, I stopped and thought: Did you just write that? You, who know nothing?

I was able to answer yes because one way to know nothing and still be able to write about the care and feeding of something is to copy information off the back of a sack of corn meal you just bought at the grocery store. What you are doing is superfluous, I thought. That was certainly true enough, but even at the callow age of twenty-two some instinct told me that superfluity might well be my pathway to success.

This seemed to be borne out a week later when I got a hurried note from the travel-weary publisher who said he read my manuscript the moment he got off the plane. He not only told me that he wanted to buy the book, but he asked me how much for the whole ball of wax. I was joyous but thrown off. Like any writer, I thought I should be told what I'm getting paid and feel lucky for any little crumb. A writer *submits*, I thought. An editor *accepts*. I decided that this fellow must think I was older, had really been around, a notion I thought I could maintain by keeping out of sight and doing everything through the mail.

After conferring with my man and then my wife, I asked for seven hundred and fifty dollars. This was *three times* what my man usually got from his publisher for a comparable manuscript; but, as he pointed out, he got forty percent of every book he sold in his store, and his life's motto was "a book with every bird." Also when I had asked him what "ball of wax" meant, he smiled and said, "Pictures." He didn't take pictures himself for his books, so of course I should be paid more for providing my own. Amazingly, my wife had had a whole change of heart when she saw the letter from New York. She quickly agreed to do the job for a third of the money. "Won't you be afraid?" I asked. She answered in an avaricious tone that shocked me: "There's *nothing* I wouldn't do for two hundred and fifty bucks."

I had no sooner agreed to a short deadline when

fate stepped in and I found myself in an odious dying in-law situation. This was a *distant* dying in-law, and why I had to go all the way to Minnesota and hover like a vulture over this poor, shriveled, oblivious octogenarian I had never even met still galls me twenty years and two marriages later. By the time the grisly business was over, two weeks had gone by and we returned home with nothing more written, no pictures taken, and the deadline only ten days away.

"Thank God you're back!" our landlady cried when we showed up to retrieve Tommy. "Here, take him. I'll never take care of anybody's bird again." As she handed the cage to me, little Tommy was down at the bottom, listless, looking about half the size he had when we left. "I don't know what happened," she sobbed. "I did everything you told me. He just wouldn't eat. He screamed his head off for over a week, then got down there and hasn't made a sound since."

It would be easy to drag out the saga of my Tommy's death—the way I found him on his side a few days later like a wide-eyed toy. Even after twenty years, I remember it as a wrenching experience. But the death of a so-called dwarf parrot who briefly perched and squawked and ate and crapped on this particular speck of dust in the universe must take its place along with everything else. The facts are enough: he starved to death—pined away for me, I'm convinced—and was buried in a Folger's coffee can.

The important point to this chronicle is not that he died, but that I continued to write about him as though he were alive. His death even enhanced the book in that I was now able to warn of the dangers of taking a vacation when you own a dwarf parrot. I hadn't yet written the chapter called "Taming, Training and Teaching to Talk," and without Tommy I had to make most of it up. It may have been an advantage in that I wasn't at all sure the bird was trainable—or, if he was, that I could have done the job.

Letting my phobic wife go into an aviary full of birds to take their pictures was like letting a normal person go into a cage full of lions. My man had to lock her in to keep the birds from escaping, and all I can say is that her greed caught up with her. There were hundreds of small parrot-like birds in there, all wild, and they began to careen up and down the length of the cage, seeming to suck out all the air with their wings. She held up for a while, but started shrieking when a bird snagged in her hair, and we had to let her out. As you might imagine, what pictures she did take weren't much good. In fact, the publisher returned them with a curt note saying they were the worst he had ever seen. (We found out later just how hard it is for anybody to photograph birds. The best technique seems to be to shoot them in a studio after they are dead and stuffed.)

Despite everything, it wasn't until the book was finished that my troubles truly began. My wife's failure to provide competent photographs delayed publication so that we missed the dwarf parrot selling season. So, without any pressure on the publisher to get the book out, the manuscript wound up being shelved without my having been paid. Be patient, my man advised, and I was—for six whole months.

Then I got a letter which I was sure contained a check. It didn't, of course. Paychecks in the publishing world are different from other paychecks in that they are almost always late—and not by mere days or even weeks, either; often years go by before you get one, and sometimes you don't get paid at all.

What was in the envelope, it turned out, was a letter from a new editor saying he had found in an old file a query from me about a possible book on dwarf parrots. The time was now right he felt, and he wanted me to proceed with the book at once. He finished by asking if I could provide photos as well.

By now, my man and I had parted company. Once the book had been finished, we slowly quit seeking one another out. (The last word I ever had from him was a late-night call from the Texas coast, wanting me to commission sailors to smuggle birds up from Argentina.) So now I was left to deal with any little publishing snafus on my own. Shakily, I wrote the new editor a letter filling him in—and to his credit he got right back with an apology. Indeed, he said, the manuscript was safely in hand, but they still couldn't proceed without pictures. And without pictures, he stated coldly, a book like this isn't worth the paper it's written on.

In other words, I was still mere filler between pictures. Am I a fool to go on? I wondered. Probably, I decided. But it occurred to me that much if not most of all writing everywhere might just be filler between something or other. If that was true, with a little work I might have just what it takes to make it big in the world of publishing.

Yet another year went by without publication, and I decided to go back to college and see if studying to be a writer might help. I wanted to go to the famous University of Iowa Writers' Workshop, but needed tuition money. On a whim I wrote the publishing company saying that I would let them have the dwarf parrot book for a flat two hundred bucks. Then they could use the extra money to buy some good pictures.

I've never been sure why, but the long shot worked. The speed at which they went into action was dizzying after what I had been used to. Within days, I had my money. Within weeks the book was in production. Then in less than two months my ten free copies came in the mail. I checked and, sure enough, the book was in the stores.

The cover was sensational, the color reproduction impeccable throughout. And on the back was a real bonus: they had advertised a book penned by Robert Stroud, the Birdman of Alcatraz, thus lending my work credibility by association.

But there were drawbacks. Scattered throughout this book about dwarf parrots were pictures of birds as big as dogs—birds like Amazons and cockatoos and African Greys. The cover, glorious as it was, was illustrated with a picture of the wrong kind of bird. The one principal Halfmoon in the book—Tommy's stand-in—had a grotesque overgrown beak and was shot in grainy black and white.

The most interesting thing to me was that the title now made no sense. Instead of *Halfmoons and Other Dwarf Parrots*, it read *Halfmoons and Dwarf Parrots*. Far from being upset, I thought it sounded like a surrealist novel, and I put it on my resume to the Writers' Workshop.

By keeping the book under wraps at Iowa and making cryptic references to it, I created a certain mystique about myself. The rumors about the book, along with basic self-promotional techniques I picked up from my teachers, helped me earn the school's coveted Fiction Writing Fellowship. Such things at Iowa carry weight in New York, and before I knew it my career was launched: I had a contract for a first novel with a prestige publisher—and the novel hadn't even been written yet. So far everything had been done on little more than rumor and promise, but now I hoped to show the world that I had what it takes.

My little first book has gotten around over the years. I've seen it myself in London and have heard that it's available in Canada, Australia, and even parts of the Orient. It's never been reviewed, I'm sure, but one big pet store can move a hundred books with a hundred birds every season. Figure how many pet stores over the country have been doing that every year for twenty years and the sales become astronomical. The book, by the way, just went into yet another edition. It's printed in Hong Kong now—the place to go for good yet cheap color reproduction of giant parrots—and sells for four times the original price. It is sealed in plastic, like pornography.

If I had played my cards right and asked for royalties, I might be a rich man today, but as it is all I got was the glory. For years after I became legitimate, more or less, I hid the fact that I had once written in such a low-level genre. But then I realized that people are charmed when you talk about humble beginnings, so I dragged it out of the closet and now use it for party entertainment.

Looking back, I can say that I accomplished what any writer must with his first book. I made something out of nothing. This phenomenon is central to the world of the printed word, but it is little understood. It can be almost impossible to do in the beginning— yet if the element of reputation ever becomes involved then something can start coming out of nothing all the time. For instance, in the little town of Cedar Hill, Texas, where I live, I recently became not only famous but venerated.

On an off-day, I went in the local library and let it be known that I was a writer. The librarian—a would-be writer herself and a person after my own heart—saw a story in my impromptu appearance, and she wrote it up for the Cedar Hill paper. The title of her piece was something like *Local Author Visits Library*. At the end of the story, she listed my book on dwarf parrots along with an impressive number of other publications most of which I hadn't written. My common name, which I had considered a curse, had finally turned to my advantage. The last book on the list was *The Biography of William Allen, 1806–1879*. It should say autobiography, of course, and the dates are a little off, but the wonderful thing is that nobody noticed. My mail now gets special handling at the post office. I get free drinks at all the local bars. And almost every weekend a young writer will cruise my gate, hoping I'll tell him how to get his first big break in the world of books.

A Whole Society of
Loners and Dreamers

On Sunday afternoons in Cedar Hill, Texas, if you're tired of taking walks in the country and fighting off the green-bellied hogflies, your next best choice is thumbing magazines at the downtown drugstore. One Sunday when I ran out of anything else to thumb, I started looking through one of those magazines geared toward helping new writers achieve success. I used to pore over them a lot when I was a teenager, and the first thing I noticed was that the ads haven't changed much over the past quarter of a century.

"IMAGINE MAKING $5,000 A YEAR WRITING IN YOUR SPARE TIME! Fantastic? Not at all. . . . Hundreds of People Make That Much or More Every Year—and Have Fun Doing It!"

"TO PEOPLE WHO WANT TO WRITE FOR PROFIT BUT CAN'T GET STARTED. Have You Natural Writing Ability? Now a Chance to Test Yourself—FREE!"

"I FIRE WRITERS . . . with enthusiasm for developing God-given talent. You'll 'get fired' too with my 48-lesson home study course. Over-the-shoulder coaching . . . personalized critiques! Amazing sales opportunity the first week. Write for my FREE STARTER KIT."

The ad that struck me the most showed a picture of a handsome and darkly serious young man sitting on a hill, picking his teeth with a weed, and gazing out over the countryside. The caption read: DO YOU HAVE THE "FAULTS" THAT COULD MEAN YOU WERE MEANT TO BE A WRITER? The ad went on to list the outstanding characteristics of writers. They are dreamers, loners, bookworms. They are too impractical, too intense, too idealistic.

When I was fourteen and had just started trying to write, I saw an ad much like this and was overwhelmed by it. That fellow on the hill was just like me, I thought. It was a tremendous feeling to discover that I might not be alone—that there was a whole society of loners and dreamers, that they were called writers, and that by sending off for a free writing IQ test I could find out by return mail if I qualified to climb the hill and chew straw with them.

I took the test and blew the top off it. The writing school said I demonstrated a rare creative potential unlike anything they had seen in years. They did wonder, though, if I had what it took to stick with them through long months of arduous training to develop my raw talent. If I really did have that kind of fortitude, the next step would be to send in some actual samples of my writing.

Spurred, I sent off everything I had ever written— two stories about 200 words each. One was about some unidentified creatures who lived in dread of an unidentified monster who came around every week or so to slaughter as many of them as he could. Some of the persecuted creatures had the option of running, hopping, scurrying, or crawling to safety, but the others, for some unexplained reason, couldn't move and had to just stand there and take it. There was a description of the monster's roaring approach. Then the last line hit the reader like a left hook: "The lawn mower ran swiftly over. . . ."

The other story I have preserved these many years:

THE RACE

Two gleaming hot rods stand side by side, poised and tensed—eager to scream down the hot asphalt track, each secretly confident that he will be the supreme victor. The time is drawing close now; in just a few minutes the race will be on.

There is a last minute check of both cars . . . everything is ready. A yell rings out for everyone to clear the track. The flagman raises the starting flag above his head, pauses for a second, and with a downward thrust of the flag, he sends the cars leaping forward with frightening speed.

They fly down the track, side by side, neither able to take the lead. They are gaining speed with every second. Faster and faster they go, approaching the halfway mark with incredible momentum. . . .

Wait! Something is wrong—one of the cars is going out of control and skidding toward the other car! The rending sound of ripping metal and sliding tires cuts through the air as the two autos collide and spin crazily off the track.

For a moment the tragic panorama is hidden by a self-made curtain of dust, but it isn't a second before the curtain is pulled away by the wind, revealing the horrible sight. There are the two hot rods, one turned over, both broken and smashed. All is quiet. . . .

Two small children, a boy and a girl, get up from

the curb where they have been sitting. They eye each other accusingly as they walk slowly across the street where the two broken toy cars lay silent. . . . "Woman driver," grumbles the little boy.

THE END

The correspondence school's copy desk quickly replied that the writing samples confirmed my aptitude test results and that they looked forward to working with me to the point of publication and beyond. I couldn't imagine what could be beyond publication but finally figured out they meant to handle my work later as agent-representative. They praised my choice of subject matter, sense of drama, and powerful surprise endings—all of which they said indicated I could sell to the sci-fi market. This made sense, because science fiction was all I had ever read voluntarily except for *Classic Comics* and, as a child, *Uncle Wiggily*. The school was particularly impressed by my style, which they said was practically poetry, in places. They made reference to my use of alliteration ("rending sound of ripping metal") and of metaphor ("self-made curtain of dust . . . pulled away by the wind").

They were quick to make clear, however, that what I had here were only germs of stories. They needed to be expanded to publishable lengths and had to have better character development—particularly the one about the bugs and grass being slaughtered by the lawn mower. They said a good writer could give even an insect an interesting personality.

The next step was to send them ten dollars for each of the two stories—the standard fee for detailed, over-the-shoulder copy-desk criticism. Then after the stories had been redone and rushed off for publication,

I should enroll in their thirty-six-lesson course, in which I would be taught the ins and outs of plotting, characterization, point of view, theme, tone, and setting. The fee was ten dollars a lesson, and after my successful completion of the course they would then handle my literary properties, protect my legal rights, etc., for the regular 10 percent.

At this point I began to wonder if I might be going in over my head. I was getting only a dollar a week from my folks and didn't understand half of what the writing school was talking about. In English class I had heard of such terms as "alliteration," "tone," and "point of view" but had no clear idea what they meant. Also I felt like an imposter. I had given my age as twenty-one. Of course, I was strutting because at fourteen I was doing better than anybody they had worked with in years, but I wondered if I could keep it up. "Rending sound of ripping metal" was genius, but could I crank out lines like that on a daily basis? I decided to try.

First I wrote them that I was a little short of cash this month and asked if, just to get started, it would be all right to work on one story for ten dollars instead of two for twenty dollars. They replied that that would be fine—just send in the ten bucks so they could get rolling.

Meanwhile I hadn't been able to get even that much money together. I approached my family and was turned down flat because my grandfather thought there was something unhealthy about people who wanted to write. He was bothered by the school's remark that my writing was like poetry. "If you were a girl, it might be different," he said, and showed me a copy of *Men's Adventure.* "Look here, why don't you get one of these two-ninety-eight worm ranches? Or one of these small-game boomerangs?"

After a few days of trying to drum up work around the neighborhood, I realized I wasn't going to be able to pull it off and decided just not to write back. But in a week I got a curt note saying they wanted to help me, were trying to be patient, but I was going to have to be more responsible. They said that writing was 1 percent inspiration and 99 percent perspiration and wondered if in my case the figures might be reversed.

This both goaded and scared me. I wrote back that on account of unexpected medical expenses I could afford to give them only five dollars at first. Could they possibly let me have a cut rate? They replied that it was strictly against their policy, but in view of my undeniably vast potential the copy-desk team had voted to go along with me just this once—send the five dollars.

By mowing lawns and selling bottles, I had by this time scraped together three dollars, but there my earning potential dropped sharply. Another week went by, and I made only forty-eight cents more. Then a letter arrived stamped in red, front and back: URGENT! IMPORTANT! DO NOT DISCARD! It said I had violated an agreement based on mutual trust and had exactly twenty-four hours to send in the five dollars. Without exactly spelling it out, they gave the impression that legal action might be taken. The letter ended: "Frankly, Mr. Allen, we're about at our wits' end with you."

I was hurt as well as shaken. I felt that I just didn't have what it takes. If there ever had been a chance of my climbing that hill and sitting with that elite group of loners and dreamers, it was gone now. I had my mother write them that I had suddenly been struck down with polio and was unable even to write my name, much less take their course. I hung onto the little money I had in case I had to give it to them to avoid a lawsuit, but I didn't hear from them after that. In a few weeks I relaxed and mailed off for the $2.98 worm ranch.

Among the
Lofty Texas Literati

When I became a writer—supposedly a solitary occupation—I thought my speech-giving days were over, but I couldn't have been more wrong. People want to see what writers look like, as well as read what they write, and lately I've been giving more talks than ever. I don't have to say yes when I'm invited to speak, but so far I always have. I feel flattered that somebody wants to hear what I have to say. It makes me think of myself as a minor leader of men.

Still, I've never much liked to give speeches, partly because I am haunted by the memory of a speech class in grade school. On the first day we gave our little talks, a poor homely fat girl went to the front of the room, smiled at us a moment, then toppled over backwards. To our horror, she cracked the hardwood floor with the back of her head and vomited two feet into the air. At the time, I had the clear sense that I could have done the same thing—and I believe I still could. The fact that I've muddled through half a lifetime of speeches without once falling from the podium does nothing to assuage this fear.

Texas has an inexhaustible number of writing groups. I am a grateful member of one, the Texas Institute of Letters, an august group of some two hundred champions including Max Apple, Donald Barthelme, and Larry McMurtry. When the other writing groups in Texas want to be addressed, they frequently turn to members of the Institute for speakers. (When the Institute wants to be addressed, it usually speaks to itself.)

I've spoken to fellow Institute members—actually a fairly modest, mild-mannered group overall—about the issue and have come up with what may be a little-known truth: I'm not alone in my dislike of giving speeches. Almost nobody, except politicians and similar types who don't know any better, likes to give speeches. I think audiences over the earth operate under the illusion that the person up there on stage thrives on what he's doing. The person in the audience, then, who knows *he* sure wouldn't thrive up there, must come away feeling that he doesn't have what it takes to be a leader of men.

I want to dispel that notion. The person in the audience probably *isn't* a leader of men, but it has nothing to do with giving speeches. Speeches are as unnatural for people as going on talk shows, and everybody ought to know it. Then maybe we could relax and just go for walks in the country, like we're supposed to do.

The last group I addressed had a name like the International League of North American Pen Women (Southwestern Branch). Nothing about the speech was unusual. I had to give it, as always, at a place I wasn't familiar with—a busy downtown place where it was hard to figure out where I was and where to park; then I had to walk too far in the heat and, strangely, in gale-force winds that almost blew me back home; then I further exhausted and unnerved myself by carrying a box of my old books I hoped to sell to supplement my tuna casserole lunch.

However late all this made me, League business was still under way when I arrived, and I had to wait too long to be introduced. But none of my nervousness showed, because I was seated, and sitting down is what I am meant to do with my life. During those long moments, I'm sure I must have appeared both casual and reflective—not modest at all, yet struck with the gravity of my responsibility and obviously equal to it.

Then I heard my name and what I hoped was enthusiastic clapping, so I got up and approached the lectern. At this moment, time speeded up and motion slowed down. The tiny rational part of me remaining knew I knew my stuff. Else why would I have been there? These people had paid money to hear me, even if I wasn't getting much of it. But who did they think I was? Could it be that I was really famous in a specialized sort of way? My shrinking rational being said no, then vanished.

Going up the steps of the stage, I seemed to be moving in an unwelcome dream that had no content, only a mood that was yellow-green and had a loud hum. (I think getting up to give a speech is what it's like to be insane.) Then I was actually behind the lectern, where I began experiencing alternating waves of panic and calm which were speeded up to about one-second intervals; I knew from the past that it was very important to catch one of the calm waves and use it to launch the speech. As I gazed down on the upturned, expectant faces, I also knew I must say something humorous and unrehearsed, or start off with a question. A question would seem peculiar to this International League of North American Pen Women, but not nearly as peculiar as firing a pistol into the air, or other strong measures people have taken to make their audience more nervous than they are.

I had been afraid all along that they would make me use a microphone, and sure enough they did. The electronics and acoustics and my distance from the mike were all right, but my voice kept bouncing back at me. It sounded as bad as it had over the tape recorder I used to practice on—even worse, because now it was conducting a personal battle with hysteria, the warring sounds of which filled the auditorium.

This is when some speakers run sobbing off the stage, go crazy, have heart attacks, or—like the poor homely fat girl from my past—faint and throw up on themselves. Of these choices, the last seemed preferable, because a few Pen Women were bound to throw up too, and cause a chain reaction throughout the whole auditorium—which is exactly what should have happened to them for asking me to give a speech in the first place.

But nothing like that occurred. The speech moved as though on its own through to the end. That endless looming future event, which took untold hours of worry and preparation, then went momentarily into a present reality (the toll of which is hard to measure, since it didn't kill me), had now quickly switched into the past. What I should have been left with was a grisly memory, but instead it became a feeling of euphoria, born of relief.

At the lunch afterward, I at first assumed that the talk was just terrible, but then somebody said how good it was (they're told to do that). I was doubtful at first, but I kept getting compliments until I began to believe them. I was even lucky enough to be offered a drink, and once it was in my hand I started fishing. "Actually, I was a little nervous," I said to a Pen Woman.

"Really?" she said. "You're the most relaxed speaker I've ever seen. And the most engaging. In fact, I want you to speak to my own little group sometime."

I smiled, feeling the euphoria close in. "Of course," I said. "Anytime."

Then as I was once again thinking of myself as a leader of men—perhaps even near the top of Texas's lofty literati—another Pen Woman came up and said, "Would you consider looking at my manuscript on psychic cats?"

Mentors and Protégés

I don't know how somebody as reclusive and misanthropic as I can be winds up involved in a burgeoning creative writing program at one of the most populated universities in the country. It is one of those incongruities that keep life exciting in a sobering sort of way. I do best observing things that don't mind being observed, like plants and animals. Pitched among people, I still observe—I can't help it—but am viewed as mordant and acerbating and, it has been suggested, less than fair.

Concerning the teaching of creative writing, I have observed two things. First, it's become an industry not unlike that of the mass production of American chickens. Second, when writers get around other writers, their writing gets confused with sex. Whole careers are made out of the mixup, and these days, as a part of affirmative action, it is by-and-large the careers of women that are made. It would be a dull world without such anomalies, and what follows are my notes on how the unlikely process works.

Those of us involved in any of the great creative writing factories already know how the young woman as literary lion got her start. She was around thirty and married and morose when she took a night class in how to write a short story. There it soon unfolded that she was smart and talented and perceptive beyond the comprehension of her earthbound friends and relatives.

She worked compulsively. Every story she wrote was better than her last. Then in front of her class-mates' fearful eyes one of her stories was published in *The Atlantic*—or was it *The New Yorker*? At any rate, it didn't turn out to be the freak occurrence a lot of people hoped for. One success led to another, mak-ing her then obviously dwarfed classmates suicidal and murderous. In just a few years she went from having block parties to waiting to be on "Cavett" where she planned to smoke cigarettes and talk dirty.

In literary households her name is a household word, yet she has too many contemporaries for me to single her out. In fact, there are so many of her these days that the real question is how this phenomenon continues to proliferate. As with most literary figures, publishers must promote each one as unique, but their teachers like to talk about them as a type. These pro-fessors generalize and oversimplify shamefully, yet their collective view has the ring of truth, if not truth itself. As one of them, I apologize to all the honorable mentors, protégés, and husbands of the world who would never dream of doing what I am about to describe.

First, the phenomenon has three psychosexual components: a cautious husband, a reckless mentor, and the young woman's own dualistic personality which consumes them both and then somehow creates literature. If Madame Bovary were alive in the United States today, she wouldn't read novels and then take arsenic—she would write a best-seller and thrive.

The cautious husband—often a lawyer or computer expert or garden variety administrator—is an unlikely victim. He's tight as a tick with the family budget but spends a fortune on his cameras and rare coins. He won't discuss much of anything—especially marital problems—with his wife, but spends galling hours chatting with the neighbors, all of whom love him for the relatively decent and perfectly domesticated male he is. In the marriage he's often domineering and controlling, though in some cases it's done in a passive sort of way. He should be given credit for believing in most of the eternal verities—and for controlling any personal demons as well. All this, however, eventually makes his wife fat and depressed, but still locked in her memory is a dream of all the books she once wanted to write. Then there's a new night class ready to start, and the cautious husband—doubtless viewing this as harmless therapy—makes a big mistake: he lets her sign up.

The energy she immediately harnesses in the name of art transcends a mere Michener or a John Jakes or any of those other writers who just know how to put in an honest day's work. To find a comparison for the young woman's exuberance, we almost have to think of a last-minute reprieve from Death Row. Powered by this unexpected second chance, her withered libido also springs back to life, starved and insatiable, and is directed at her creative writing teacher.

The quickly cuckolded husband usually views his

WILLIAM ALLEN

wife's professor as a dissolute lecher preying on the fantasies of his susceptible students, and this may be quite true. The impurity of their intent varies, but in the end doesn't matter. All that matters is the emergence of the she-lion of literature.

The transition is as marked as the dividing of an amoeba. At home she still appears to be a deferring housewife clinging to her spouse for the security he offers. But at the university—in class at first, then in private conference over drinks afterwards—she is animated and spirited and has disquieting sexual feelings whenever she discusses literature. She has lascivious fantasies about her teacher which—since psychosexual matters overshadow reason—soon are confessed for the good of her art. As their relationship grows, her relationship with her husband wanes—though she won't dump him until all three are driven half-mad by her ambivalence.

Her commitment to her mentor has a heightened reality and borders on hysteria. She works so hard to please him that she is nearly driven to exhaustion and nervous collapse. The teacher is just as over-zealous in his capacity as editor and critic; in fact if she did collapse he would probably finish her story for her.

The mentor is the only one who has enough experience with all this to be objective, yet he remains helpless to temper the process. He fantasizes a lasting involvement with this Marilyn Chambers of literature, a creature with a face as pure as Ivory Snow but who writes like the devil herself. Yet his fears are tapped as well, and he views his protégé as more demented and destructive than she really is. He fears her implicit madness and finds it irresistible. To him, she is the quintessence of the forbidden. She will betray him, drive him insane, ruin his writing, and call him at home. It is true that she can be obsessive and occasionally out of control, and at times this appropriately terrifies him. Then it drives him to fantasies of escaping together, of plunging into the heart of darkness— across the border, say, into the jungle in search of Mayan codices that will unlock the secrets of heaven and hell.

His fears, at least, are real. At the same time protégés adore their mentor, the admiration verges on envy. They don't want his power, exactly, but at least want power of their own. In the end, very few will ever dedicate a book to him.

No matter what, she will succeed without him. Whereas she once felt at his mercy for guidance, she soon has half of New York's editorial elite ready to guide her. Her need for her mentor and husband vanishes at roughly the same time and, free of both, she works even harder. After that, it all happens quickly. Her first book is an overnight success, of course, but along with it she is also offered a high-paying position at one of the best-known creative writing schools in the country.

The future of the mentor is not so certain. Some may cling to the end, be cuckolded themselves, cast off ignominiously, become drunken bums, and die in the gutter. But the wise ones always know to exit like Svengali at the precise moment that will leave the protégé slightly crushed and, whenever she's back in town, cruising his house at midnight.

The Last Strand: Lament of a Balding Man

One day when I was a sophomore in college, my gloating roommates presented me with a Baggie full of my own precious hair, all in little matted circles about the size of Norelco coffee filters. It was solid evidence that I was the cause of our clogged drain, but, plumbing aside, I maintained that it was only natural that I would shed a lot. I told my roommates: "I've got more hair than both of you skinheads put together."

Nevertheless, what began that day has now amounted to over twenty years of preoccupation with hair loss. *Dear God*, I used to pray (and I was serious), *just give me time to marry and establish a career. Just give me till thirty.*

By thirty I wasn't anywhere near bald, but I was watching my grandfather with a new eye. He was spending his twilight years in his rocker, watching the radio, missing the coffee-can spittoon between his legs, dozing, and allowing his bald head to be used as a heliport by the two family parakeets. He didn't care or even seem to notice when they fluttered down onto his dome, fondly preened his horseshoe-shaped fringe, and then dozed along with him. He was my mother's father—on the side of the family we supposedly inherit baldness from—and I remembered that all my mother's brothers were bald, too. Some of them had lost their hair in their early twenties. Grandfather liked to tell how Uncle Jack shaved his head, having been told his hair would grow back thicker, but it never grew back at all. Jack was a real bastard; still, I hated the idea of somebody throwing away his last years of hair like that.

And I was watching these poor old fellows on the streets who would let their side hair grow long and part it down near their *ears* and comb a few strands up over their bald heads. They looked just awful, yet why couldn't they see that themselves? I decided it was like gradually getting fat—we keep seeing ourselves in the mirror the way we looked when we were thin. So, when our hair starts to go, we lower the part just a little, maybe by accident at first, and the difference it makes is so wonderful that we start doing it all the time. And at first it really does work. But if our hair continues to thin and our part continues to move on down, then the habit becomes a vice. Pretty soon people can tell what we're doing, but we think it's still looking good—or at least we think it's a good trade-off. Carry such self-delusion to its logical end, and what you wind up with is a half dozen two-foot-long hairs hideously combed and glued onto a shiny bald pate. Once I had this figured out, I swore it would never happen to me.

Then one day an old college compadre came through town. When he left me and my hangover, he also left behind an unfamiliar, nameless little plastic container full of something terribly pink and thick and tacky to the touch. Now, I'd been around enough to know that what had been accidentally left to me was some sort of *hair conditioner*.

I couldn't resist. I put the stuff all over my head.

Even as I rubbed it in I could feel my hair getting gloriously thicker. And once it was dry and combed, it seemed as though I had twice as much hair. Then, after a few days, just to see, I used more conditioner and, sure enough, I wound up with what seemed like four times as much hair. But mere days had passed and the bottle was already half gone, so I called my friend and he gave me not only the name of the stuff but also the name of a companion product that you put on after you wash your hair, which seems to give you *eight* times as much hair. You buy the stuff by the gallon through the mail, and, he said, for best results you comb the companion product in, making sure every hair is coated, and then you blow-dry to keep the hairs from sticking together. I quickly ordered one gallon of each product, bought a Conair Pro Style 1200 blow dryer, and for a while I felt like a new man. What had really happened, though, without my real-izing it, was something terribly aberrant: I had fallen victim to *the vice of artifice*.

The problem was that even after all those applica-tions, after all that time spent, and even though I would leave my bathroom mirror looking good, I didn't *stay* looking good. Even though each strand of hair was thicker, my hair en masse wasn't thicker at all. If I wanted, I could make every hair as thick as nails, but no matter what the thickness, there was still space between the hairs. So I really was trying to get one hair to do the work of, say, four or five, and it just couldn't do it. Even with a solid coat of hair spray, the wind could undo in seconds the efforts of an hour. And if I just stayed inside—which I was doing more and more of now—the hairs soon would sort of collapse, and my head would actually seem to get smaller.

One day I just washed my hair like a normal person and didn't put anything on it, and I was shocked at how thin on top I had gotten. I had been camouflaging so long that the change was too abrupt for me to bear, and there was nothing to do but order yet more gallons of thickener and conditioner. By now I was reading with interest what used to seem like obviously exploitative ads. Only rarely would I think: *Why such a big deal? Why can't I adjust?*

More years passed and, after having my hair cut at home by wives or girlfriends for longer than I could remember, I suddenly found myself forced into the streets to find a barbershop. I just drove around and stopped at the first one I saw. This barbershop had two barbers. One was a silent fellow who sat in his barber chair hooked over a hamburger, and the other was Mick the Barber, a short fellow full of nervous energy, who had a head of hair that made me think of *Planet of the Apes*. To my knowledge, I had never seen a toupee in person, so I didn't immediately think of Mick's swept-back gorillalike bush as made out of Taiwanese synthetic fiber.

"Just a trim," I said. "Nothing off the top." A case might be made that there was nothing to *take* off the top, but it wouldn't really be true. There was still some. At least I thought there was, except maybe for right up front. It certainly *looked* as if I had hair up there, anyway. But Mick the Barber wasn't fooled. He stood

WILLIAM ALLEN

back, seeming perplexed, walked around, and studied my head from various angles. "I got to figure out
where all this is coming from," he said, and did exactly
what I didn't want him to do. He started running his
comb all over my head, undoing all my morning's
work, snagging his comb on congealed hair spray,
pulling out, I feared, yet more precious hair. "Jesus,
look at this!" he said, holding up a shock of hair
growing from the back of my head. "It must be a foot
and a half long!" Then his voice took on an intimate
tone that was both brotherly and covert. "Let me ask
you something. Have you ever considered a hairpiece?" "No," I said, sort of in shock but also *relieved*,
because here I was being dragged out of the closet,
being forced for the first time to talk to somebody about
my problem with hair. "But I have thought about a
transplant."

"Let me show you something," Mick said. He hustled off and returned with a hairy clump in his hand
about the size of a mouse, but a mouse not of this
earth, because it had fur at least six inches long, and
he pressed it onto my scalp, up front, where it somehow stuck. Then he twirled me around so I could look
in the mirror behind me. What I saw made me want
to cry. It was as though I had been twirled ten years
back in time, except now all my pimples were gone.
"Haven't seen that much hair in a long time, have
you?" Mick said, standing beside me, looking into the
mirror with me, like a brother. What I needed, he told
me as we both gazed at my reflection, wasn't a toupee at all. I just needed one of these little pieces, or,
as they are called in the trade, sliders. Of all the ways
to have more hair, the slider was the best. It was the
easiest to use and maintain, the least detectable, the

most natural. I could throw away the hair spray. I could play tennis and even go swimming and never worry again.

"I bet you just hate it when the wind comes up, don't you?" Mick said. Then he started cutting my hair. He cut it too short, it turned out, and I went home looking awful. I called him up and griped about the lousy haircut for a while. Then I made an appointment to be fitted for a slider.

We met at night, like rats or roaches, and the barbershop at that hour came into its own. I felt sleazy, too, but I kept thinking that I could stop at any time, that all I had to lose was seventy-five bucks—which shows you how little I understood the vice of artifice.

First Mick clipped precious samples of my front hair and put them into three envelopes marked LEFT SIDE, RIGHT SIDE, and CENTER, so the slider could be made to match in color, texture, and wave. I practically knew every one of those clipped hairs by *name,* and when Mick noticed how miserable I looked, he said, "Believe me, at this point a few more hairs just doesn't matter." Then he made a sort of mold of my head out of paper and masking tape and drew on it with a pen the boomerang shape of the slider, which was to be about an inch wide and three inches long. "Hairlines are three fingers' width from the top of the eyebrows," he said, measuring. Judging from where his fingers were, I would have the same apelike hairline he did, and I measured for myself. "Mick, my hairline's *four* fingers." I told him I thought the idea was that everything was supposed to be exactly the same, except there would be more hair. "Okay," he said. "I'll go four fingers and even draw in a little recede. What the hell!"

The slider arrived three weeks later, and when Mick took it out of the box, it looked like enough hair for three or four people. "We cut it," he explained. "We thin it out, just like real hair. The only difference is we go real slow, 'cause this hair don't grow back!" He held the slider up to the light. "Synthetic is best. It lasts longer and it looks more real than human hair. They make these in Taiwan, by hand. They insert each little hair individually into the lace."

Then he put the slider against my head and frowned. "Hey, fella, you been out in the sun?" What he meant, of course, was that the piece was a different *color* than it was supposed to be. But then he decided it wasn't so bad after all. "Hell, once your own hair is combed through, it'll look great."

Mick had a little artist in him, anyway, I think, or he wanted to, and *I* sure wanted him to. I took heart in the way he moved around the chair, holding the piece in place and looking again and again. "Okay," he said finally, "now I'm gonna shave the hair off the front of your head. You can't put hair on top of hair. It don't adhere right, and it'll just pull your real hair out anyway." He didn't take much off—he didn't *have* to—but the little that did go made a lot of difference. "Don't worry about it," he said. "Once we get the slider on, you'll feel like a new man."

My particular kind of hairpiece was stuck on with tape. The double-sided transparent tape came in rolls, and it had to be cut in exactly the shape of the transparent plastic base holding the lace that held the synthetic hair. Mick spent three hours trimming and shaping the hair and cutting new tape, and he stuck the slider on me at least a hundred times. At the end we both were exhausted but we thought it looked good. Mick said, "Call me tomorrow. We can tell better in the light of day." It didn't take that long. I went straight home to my bathroom mirror, and it looked horrible.

But after three days of Mick refining the piece—thinning it, mostly—I finally looked good even in my own mirror, and on the evening of the fourth day I went public. At a dinner party, a woman who was sort of brassy anyway looked at me and said, "What did you do to your hair? Get a toup?" From somewhere deep within there arose a strange, almost sociopathic calm, and I said, "Nah. I had it styled. Cost me almost twenty bucks." "Well," she said. "It looks great." To this day I'm convinced she really did believe me, and nobody else that night or afterward ever looked twice, though a few people did ask if I had lost a little weight.

In order to stay looking like a new man, I had to spend about an hour in the bathroom every morning. And then every few days I had to shave the part of my head going under the tape so it would adhere and not pull out those little hairs still trying to grow under there. For some reason I still cared about them.

If I was hung over or upset or nervous or impatient, cutting the tape was a nightmare. But, since I also had Liquid Tape, I only had to cut new tape about once a week. Personally, I thought the Liquid Tape was glue, but Mick seemed annoyed if I called it that. "It reactivates the adhesive properties of the tape," he told me, but I tried it on an old stamp one day and it reactivated that, too. I would put the stuff on my tape with a little brush like the kind they use with fingernail polish and it worked fine until the *residue* built up. The gummy crud had built up on my head, too. What I did about that was clean it off with the *solvent* that came in expensive little bottles that Mick sold along with the tape and Liquid Tape and slider shampoo.

When that was done, and I'd washed my other hair and put on all the thickeners that I still hadn't been able to give up, I was ready to place the piece. Placing the piece was like balancing a broom on one's forefinger. It was a gift, and I had it, but some days were better than others. I would try to do it in a fast, easy, fluid motion and hope I hit just right, because if I didn't the piece was stuck to my head and I'd have to prize it up with my thumb and try again.

Spending one hour to have twenty-three good ones didn't seem bad, but once a week came the hellish tape-changing time and, what with also having to shampoo and blow-dry the slider, the whole process took so long that I just scheduled it for the weekends.

Almost a year went by like that, and it was seeming *normal*, then one night there was a freak fire in my birdbath, and while I was trying to put it out, my hair melted all over my forehead. All those little individually placed Taiwanese hairs reacted to the heat in basically two ways. Some were singed and curled up on the ends like little used matchsticks. The others actually melted and bonded together in more or less solid clumps. I worked with every hair individually, separating some and cutting off the curled ends of others, then I combed my other hair through what was left and made a dash to Mick's.

He agreed that a replacement was in order, but then he said we should go for a larger piece, one that covered the whole top of my head instead of just the front. "You've thinned out a lot in the past year," he said. "It's probably all going to fall out anyway. We might as well nip it in the bud." He went on to say how worry-free a complete piece is, without all that mingling of hair to go through, and in the end I agreed.

When the toupee arrived, it was perfect, except that some hardworking Taiwanese had all the hair going the wrong way. The part was on the wrong side, and to make it work Mick tried putting the piece on my head *backward*, which was disconcerting, but it seemed to look okay, so we went ahead with it. Having the whole top of my head shaved wasn't any fun, either, but I had to admit that once we were done I looked better than ever.

The problem was that I looked too good. People wanted to *touch* me, to pat me on the head or ruffle my hair, and I had to establish a new *personal distance* between myself and everybody else. I had to stand and sit farther from everyone and still be ready to jump away or jerk my head back if somebody came at me anyway.

Then one night this guy who was thought of as sort of dumb—but I wonder—got really drunk at a party and came up behind me while I was sitting on a couch and patted me on the head. He was letting me know— this was the suggestion, anyway—that he wasn't jealous that I had briefly dated his wife years before they had even met. As he patted, something perverse in me said just to sit there on that couch and stick it out, to bluff, to dare him to notice all that lumpy lace and plastic foundation under there. "Hey," he said. "This feels like a toupee." His wife gaily cried so that the whole party could hear, "No, that's his hair, all right. I'll vouch for that!" Everybody laughed at the guy, and I was saved again.

But I knew I couldn't go on. The next day I bought a cap to cover the toupee. The cap was one somebody on a foreign fishing boat might wear, sort of Italian- or English-looking, with a little bill on it, and people thought it was cute. But meanwhile, underneath the cap and the toupee, I was letting my own hair grow back. I couldn't let it grow much without it being pulled out by the tape, of course, but I could at least get a start, then I planned to remove the toupee and let my hair finish growing in under the cap. It was a good plan, but when I took off the toupee the cap didn't fit anymore.

By this time I had remarried, and so I had a confi-dante, and that helped, but I became morbid and depressed and generally terrible to be around, any-way, and after a few weeks we decided we couldn't take it anymore and went to see about a transplant.

Doctors give transplants, and what we went to was a doctor's office with a waiting room and a reception-ist and with nurses going by, but something was wrong. It wasn't busy enough. It didn't smell anti-septic enough. The waiting room had too many plas-tic potted plants. The women working there looked wrong, too. They were too polite, and they sort of watched us, unlike in a regular doctor's office, where you have to tackle somebody to get any attention. And there was something else—a sign over the reception-ist's window that mentioned paying in advance.

An older woman in a nurse's costume came for us and had us wait for what seemed like a calculated amount of time in a little diagnostic room, then when the doctor came in I could see right away why the place looked like it did. The doctor himself didn't look real. He looked like he was just . . . I don't know—

pretending. But the thing that concerned me most was that his hair didn't look real. It wasn't growing like real hair, or it looked like hair growing in the wrong place, if that makes any sense—and that was exactly the case, because he'd had a total top-of-the-head transplant, and all that hair on top was really side or back hair, and, for some reason, hair grows differently depending on what part of the head it's on. And there was one other little item. His front hair was pulled forward as if to cover something, the way I had always covered my receding hairline. What he was covering—but not quite, because I could still see up under there a little—was a hairline that looked wrong. It looked like a little hedge or stalks of celery or anything else you can think of that's been planted in a row. It looked just awful, but *he* didn't seem to know it and offered himself as an example of what I, too, would soon look like.

He explained that process in a medical way, because, I think, to get a transplant, to feel right about a transplant, it helps to think of baldness as a *disorder* that can be handled *surgically* by the hair transplantation method. It's really a skin graft, such as you would want after, say, a burn disorder. Grafts of hair-bearing skin, or plugs, about the size of a pencil eraser and each containing six to eighteen hairs, are taken from the donor site, or that horseshoe-shaped fringe area that didn't go bald even on my grandfather. These plugs are then stuck in holes just punched in the bald part of your head for that purpose. An anesthetic is used. Some doctors will only do fifty at a time, but my doctor said he would do three hundred if somebody was in a hurry. I estimated how many plugs I would need at thirty-five dollars each, figuring my

Master Charge balance into the calculation, and thought about a hundred ought to do it. But my doctor thought six hundred minimum and maybe a thousand to do it right—in other words, a whole top-of-the-head deal like he had.

Talking as if all this was an accomplished fact, he warned that afterward I would have to be sure not to tie my shoelaces for a while. This was to avoid bleeding. I couldn't go out in the sun, and this was to avoid bleeding, too. There were lots of other things having to do with avoiding bleeding, but he told me if I started bleeding anyway I should get to a doctor fast. Then he told me that my $3,500 worth of transplanted hair was going to *fall out* in two to four weeks. But, thank goodness, in two or three months it would begin to grow in again and, given the length of my hair, which was fashionably long, it only would take about six to eight months to grow to the right length.

In the parking lot outside the doctor's office, my wife and I discussed the wisdom of going ahead with this deal. "What do you think?" she asked.

"I don't know," I said. "It's a lot of money."

"Don't worry about the money. The main thing is, do you want to do it?"

"God, I don't know. What did you think of that doctor?"

She was quiet. "Well, I picked up some bad vibes."

"Did you? So did I."

"But we can find somebody else."

"Yeah, but what if I go through all that and spend all that money and then come out looking like he does?"

She was quiet, then said, "Well, there's always electrolysis."

Instead of a transplant, I used the money to go to Puerto Vallarta, where I grew a beard and, coincidentally, tanned my scalp. I came home free at last from the vice of artifice—and with some advice for balding friends: so far, in the world of the balding man, the best thing on the market is a small vacation.

The Day My Back Went Out

M y back went out on April 13. Right up till the moment before it happened, I had been one of the blessed creatures on the planet Earth. I had been born a human of sound mind and body in the right part of the world and at just the right time to miss fighting in a war and to see man land on the moon. I was just appropriately neurotic for my century and station in life. But most important, I had, until that day, been pain-free.

It makes me sound zealous or even overwrought when I itemize everything I was doing, and maybe I was, but at the time it just felt like good healthy springtime activity. I was mowing eight acres of yard and pruning five acres of trees. I was jogging. I moved, by myself, a six-hundred-pound piano up four steps and through three rooms, using immense amounts of mind over matter, sudden bursts of explosive energy, and a Toyota car jack. Then a few days later, I impulsively knocked out a wall between the kitchen and dining room, cleaned up the mess, did some quick carpentry, and repainted.

It still seems wrong that it wasn't the six-hundred-pound piano that struck me down. That would have had a flair to it, have been a story my friends could tell to help them adjust to their loss. The remodeling, which included new shelves for the crystal, hadn't done it either. What ruined my health, apparently, was my carefully placing a delicate wine glass on one of the higher freshly painted shelves.

The pain didn't come all at once, with lightning bolts jumping out of my back, but rather like the inexorable tide. Full tide took about an hour, then I was writhing on the bed. The pain ran in the shape of a large boomerang up from my lower back to my neck, over my left shoulder and down my arm to my watch. In my ignorance, I took it like a man. I thought it would go away—and within a week it had, except for my upper arm which hurt worse than ever.

At that point, I broke down and went to a doctor—the first of six. I've always wanted to like and respect doctors, especially the older, fatherly ones. Even though I had never much needed them before, I enjoyed knowing they were there in their offices, surrounded by all their books. There are no words I want to use to express how I feel about doctors now, but I will say that I'm not bitter. Bitterness suggests being imbalanced, and if I chose to be imbalanced I would prefer to feel something such as, say, murderous.

The first doctor, who at seventy-six was fatherly all right, came highly recommended by an otherwise dependable friend. The senile old fellow raised my left arm, asked if it hurt, muttered "rheumatoid arthritis," then wrote out a three-month prescription for one of the more powerful steroids on the market. He never asked to see me again. You're supposed to monitor that poison, I found out, to see if it's going to produce any harmful side effects such as cardiac arrest. I also found out that rheumatoid arthritis can't even be diagnosed without a blood test, so I went for a second opinion.

"Fibrositis," my new doctor said, which was a catch-all term for a painful muscular condition for which there is no known cause or cure, but he gave me some anti-inflammatory medicine anyway, which upset my stomach. I knew the diagnosis couldn't be right because there was a known cause for my problem. It was the placing of that wine glass, a simple fact this doctor ignored, so he couldn't have determined if there was known cure or not.

Before I could get to a third expert, I happened to see my uncle who surprised me with an opinion of his own. "You've got a ruptured biceps tendon," he said, a condition he himself had once had. This is supposedly a rare injury in which the tendon connecting the biceps muscle to the shoulder snaps and the biceps falls in a great lump somewhere down around the elbow. The grisly malady is called the Popeye syndrome and generally befalls athletes, especially professional football players. My uncle, who is in aerospace, got his starting a lawn mower. All in all, he didn't have much credibility with me; I thought that, like most people with new and special knowledge, he probably saw ruptured biceps tendons everywhere. How he saw one on me, though—since my biceps was more or less intact—I didn't know.

But I mentioned it to the next doctor, anyway, who

said with unusual drama for a doctor, "By God, you do have one. I'm sending you to an orthopedic man."

I was excited because we seemed to have hit on a definite problem, and I dared tell the orthopedic man what was wrong with me. He responded with the impatience of that breed of doctor who believes that patients are not put on this earth to think or talk, but to do what they're good at—getting sick, getting treated, and dropping dead. "You *had* a *partial* ruptured biceps tendon," he said, "but it healed long ago." Then he had me think back till I recalled when it happened. It was in 1972, when I was arm-wrestling the ferret-like chairman of a university English department. There had been a knot on my biceps ever afterward, which I had come to be used to and even vaguely proud of because it made my muscle look bigger. "Your problem is not here," the doctor said, tapping my aching and more-or-less useless arm. "It's here." And he tapped the back of my neck, which didn't hurt at all.

I was upset, though for odd reasons, one being residual guilt from childhood over my bad posture. My posture, I was convinced, grew out of being encouraged to slouch by certain media idols of the fifties. When my parents and teachers told me not to slouch, they never said why, so I assumed it had something to do with immorality or social rebellion, if that makes any sense. Of course I soon cultivated the posture of a buzzard—though a rather handsome buzzard, I thought, with a high double pompadour.

When I asked if my problem had to do with posture, he said, "That has nothing to do with it," then added brutally: "It's called old age."

Since I was the only other person in the room, I

knew he was talking to me, but I had as much trouble understanding him as if he had lapsed into German. Since I had shown no serious signs of aging—except for a sudden siege of baldness ten years earlier—I had dimly supposed it was a state of mind; also, since I was a late bloomer in everything else I did, I think I believed that I would grow old late, too.

He put my X rays on a screen and pointed at a disc between two vertebrae at the base of my neck. He said that this disc was getting old and collapsing and calcifying, causing the vertebrae to pinch a nerve where they were grinding and pounding together everytime I moved, and that the pinched nerve triggered pain in my arm. "It's operable," he told me, then estimated that I wouldn't really need an operation until around the turn of the century. I was relieved at first, then realized he was only talking about sixteen years. Also, what did he mean by *need?* It occurred to me that I might be in for sixteen years of slow torture which would slowly escalate until I just couldn't take it anymore. What discredited him, though, was the galling suggestion that I had somehow leapfrogged into old age.

While I went to more doctors, my wife investigated the problem from a different angle. She asked her psychic, who was almost two thousand miles away in California, to take a look at my arm, and I learned that all this apparently was just a minor carry-over from when I was an Egyptian king. My medical report from back then appeared to her while in a trance, as on a newspaper, though in hieroglyphics, which she couldn't read, but luckily my guides could. (These guides are vague timeless stellar little creatures, busy as bees, assigned to get us from lifetime to lifetime in the best way possible.) They would go to work on my arm, while all I needed to do was take it easy for a while and get in lots of sauna time.

I was hesitant about the sauna idea because I am claustrophobic around water and even water-related environments such as greenhouses, but I did like the idea of taking it easy. In fact, it sounded so good that I began to wonder if I were overtaxed, so I checked with my psychiatrist. She referred me to a technician with a biofeedback machine, and he confirmed that, indeed, I was stressed—to beyond the point that his machine was willing or able to monitor. So my psychiatrist thought it couldn't hurt to take it easy for a while, but beyond that she said she would explore with me the *reasons* people become stressed—if I would like to commit to change in order to achieve a better or even self-actualized life. I told her I would consider it, but the truth was I could hardly imagine a better life, especially if it involved change. All I wanted, of course, was a better arm.

Then a beatific friend suggested transcendental meditation, which should take care of my arm, and also, for an extra fee, would allow me to levitate or walk through walls. God knows, I would love to have those skills, but my Texas upbringing was so offended by the thought of making fruit and flower offerings and having a secret mantra that I knew I would never have the proper attitude to learn them. Deep down, my fate was pitched with the scientific method, so I decided to give medical science yet another chance.

In the world of medicine, it seems uncannily common for a sick yet thorough person to search far and wide for the best specialist in a given area of pain, only to find that person in his own backyard. Inflated local reputation and a patient's vain desire to brag about his doctor might account for it, but in any case it happened to me, too. I found the best back man in the known universe right in Dallas, only sixteen miles from the little town I lived in. This fellow was head of physical medicine at a major hospital which had had a great reputation until a screw-up over the amount of radioactivity in their X rays. They took pictures of over a thousand people before they caught the problem, and for a while it was like a little Hiroshima right there in the middle of Dallas. The hospital was still poorly attended, but this genius came so highly recommended from so many different sources that, if necessary, I would have gone to see him in a leper colony on the Mosquito Coast.

I liked his look and manner—he was English with those gigantic eyebrows associated with brilliance—and he impressed me with his success rate and innovations, for sure, but what won me over was the way he embraced, instead of contradicted, almost everything I had been told so far. None of the doctors, except the one who had diagnosed rheumatoid arthritis, had been wrong. The problem was that I had everything they claimed—fibrositis, tendonitis, bursitis with a calcium spur, early osteo disintegration in the cervical vertebrae, a pinched nerve, a traumatized left arm with probable calcium deposits and scar tissue, and, finally, early osteoarthritis with spurs in the lumbar region. The last was a surprise since the only time my lower back had gone out was the hour before my last wedding, which seemed understandable at the time. His gloomy prediction, however, was that I could expect it to go out over every little thing from now on.

In short, most of the other doctors had gone to their

target in their own way and hit it, only to miss the fact that there were many targets to deal with. This was bleak news, all right, but attended by the rough comfort that comes with taking truth on the chin. The main thing was that if I did as I was told, I would be completely well in ninety days. Then, by continuing with a maintenance plan he had invented, I should lead a long, happy pain-free life. I was convinced and committed myself to his program in the fervent way one commits to marriages or training dogs, which turned out to be just what it took, too.

When I checked in as an outpatient in the hospital's physical therapy unit and took a seat in the waiting room—a kind of no-frills holding station—I immediately began to hear the tortured screams of the other patients. Out of the corner of my eye, I followed the sounds down a long hall and, to my horror, I could see a couple of my future compatriots hanging, it seemed, by their necks, their faces red and swollen, eyes squeezed shut, lips grotesquely pursed. And every few minutes a brutish physical therapist would come down the hall escorting various delirious, moaning octogenarians in green, backless hospital gowns, out on their morning walks.

Then my therapist came and led me away. After what I had just seen, I think I went only because she was so young and attractive and good at friendly conversation, unlike some of her colleagues who seemed appropriately suited to deal with hell on earth. If you've ever seen *Harvey* and remember a certain Nurse Kelly, that's who my therapist was like, more or less. It helped me to think that I would just be spending over an hour a day for two weeks with my own personal Nurse Kelly—though realistically, of course, I would be getting nothing more than twenty-minute daily doses of moist heat, twenty-five minutes of inversion therapy, ten minutes of massage, five minutes of ultrasound, and twenty minutes of traction.

We got right to work and in minutes were in what at the time I viewed as a pleasantly personal situation, behind drawn curtains, my shirt off as she slowly rubbed the ultrasound device over my Popeye syndrome. Then I had my massage which, as you might imagine, was even better than ultrasound, but after that the honeymoon was over. I was abruptly taken out into the open center of the unit, to the traction machine.

The way traction works, basically, is that you sit in something like a barber chair, with a harness around your head and jaw, while a pneumatic pump intermittently pulls your head up, putting distance between the vertebrae in your neck. When the pressure was on, I couldn't see very well, but if I tried I could see a little, and what I saw—off down the long hall I had first come down—was the waiting room with several people staring back at me in horror.

During the following two weeks, I came to view the world in a darker light, and it partly had to do with my fellow patients. We don't see people that bad off walking around on the streets—because they can't walk, for one thing, or most of them can't. Every day, they were dragged or wheeled into that hellhole from wherever it was that they were being kept out of sight, and were—so far as I could tell—tortured in the name of exercise just for having lived too long. Where, I wondered, were my contemporaries?

By the end of the treatment, my body had improved some, I think, not that I much cared anymore. I left the unit with the cervical and lumbar mobility of a cat, but now I was a demoralized cat, aged, with a mental problem as well as a physical one.

My left arm still didn't feel much better, either, though my doctor seemed pleased enough with Nurse Kelly's efforts. He decided that I should buy my own home traction machine (which he had invented) and inversion table, and matter-of-factly told me to use these items for one hour a day for the rest of my life. As I carted home the equipment and converted our bedroom to accommodate it, I kept in mind what a big factor attitude is in dealing with pain, and I vowed not to let my moodiness interfere with the daily regimen. I didn't either, except for some harmless mourning over this arm that had once written books, was remarkable at throwing darts, and that had set the world record for non-stop broom-balancing—a record that, to this day, has not been broken.

Despite my proper attitude, within a week of starting home traction, my mandible began to hurt, right at the point where my lower jaw held the harness. What that meant to me was that my teeth were being pressed and ground together for twenty minutes a day from thirty pounds of unnatural pneumatic pressure. My doctor seemed impatient with my complaint, clearly viewing teeth as trivial compared to his life's mission of separating my cervical vertebrae. He spoke of ways to "increase tolerance" and how best to "minimize damage."

He didn't know who he was talking to. I love my teeth. I have all of them, despite the relentless efforts of dentists every six months or so to pull my wisdom teeth. I have never had a cavity. Ever since my pompadour fell off a decade ago, I have depended on my teeth for charm and confidence in social situations. (Ironically, the probable reason I have wonderful teeth is that I have too much calcium in my system, which I think ultimately accounts for my bad back.)

So my confidence in my doctor was already shaken, when out of the blue I got an offer to spend two weeks in a cloud forest in far Costa Rica. My doctor was happy for me, I think, but also upset that I would be off traction for so long. In fact, he was adamant that I not be off it and told me to take along some rope, a pulley, and a giant-sized Clorox bottle. I was to fill the bottle with rocks, rig the apparatus over a limb in the jungle, and yank my neck with it for twenty minutes a day, rain or shine.

When I got off the phone, I spoke to my wife about it. "It just doesn't sound right," I told her.

My wife has a good mind, though she sometimes relies on intuition for some things I don't think you should be intuitive about, like my back. To her credit, though, she had patiently endured my alliance with my doctor. She had gone with me to get my traction machine and inversion table at a store that also sold bedpans and catheters and prosthetic devices. She had even taken instruction from Nurse Kelly and had learned to massage like a geisha.

But now something snapped. "Of course it doesn't sound right," she said. "It's insane." She swept her arm around at the physical therapy unit our once cozy bedroom had become. "All this is insane! Don't you know you're still a young man?"

I don't choose to believe that her last remark made me take her advice over that of a famous doctor. I didn't necessarily agree that my doctor was mad, either. I thought his instruction might well be a measure of his genius, pointing to a rare quality of mind that cuts through incongruity like butter. But the fact is, I went to Costa Rica without his invention and never saw that prince of back care again.

I still hurt, however, and it is not lost on me that I'm not alone. From all the commiserating stories I've heard, I believe that half of America, more or less, suffers from a bad back. And I've yet to find anyone who has found a real answer. Where are the secret cures? The healing saints? The investigations? This seems to be one area where it's every patient for himself.

In my own continuing search for a cure, I've recently eliminated hypnotism and surgery, but am still considering a better world through chemistry. A fellow at UCLA says he has had good luck administering morphine and steroid injections directly into the spine. I think he's on to something there, but it's only for extreme cases so far, which means I won't qualify till I'm, say, ninety, and ready for a whole new neck.

The only creation of science and advice from a doctor that I've benefited from so far has been the inversion table, which in the last few years has become popular among athletes and related types who build whole identities out of their good physical health. As a left-handed person with dyslexia, I seem to think better upside down and become almost philosophical when using this table. I'm a full inch taller now, too, which, if it keeps up, makes me wonder if I might not just outgrow my problem.

Living in
Other People's Houses

It's a terrible thing for a man to break up with his wife and wind up homeless on somebody else's couch. The idea of it makes civilized men shudder, and it may keep marriages together years longer than they would have otherwise. It's never stopped me, though, and after three divorces I have become an expert on what it takes to live in other people's houses.

What I have to say about the experience can, I think, stand up as advice, yet it may have no practical application. I have had grisly options available to me that you may not; if you don't have them, feel lucky and let this stand as a horrific reminder that it's a cold, wet world out there when you give up family and home.

First, I do not stay with relatives. One's life is pitched with relatives at random; the only thing we can count on with relatives is that we have nothing in common with them. Very likely they may be actively deranged. They almost certainly will be depressing reminders of our pitiful lineage. Of course, you may *have* to stay with relatives; if you do, try to find a doting grand-mother who lives with a parakeet. They will do any-thing domestic for you, asking nothing in return except perhaps companionship with Perry Mason reruns and an occasional ride to the store for snuff. They are among the last saints on earth. They are better than wives. If I still had one, I would throw myself at her feet and never stray again.

I do not stay with friends, either, though I have. I would again, I suppose, except my welcome has worn out. Friends take you in for the noblest of reasons, but who you are to them can only last in the abstract. They have a fantasy about you—that you are the pal of their youth, or that you are the same happy, pros-perous person you were when you had a wife and golden retriever. They do not appreciate the misera-ble wretch you really are. And another thing: old married people—who at my age are what we get—have strange ways of behaving to one another that no one, even a friend, should see.

I do not stay with colleagues, though as a writer this option seemed ideal to me at first. Writers can be erratic creatures, and the chances of teaming up with another one in the same boat you're in are excellent. Writers have literature as a common interest, which can be nice, but they also tend toward a common affinity for alcohol and divorce. It's just awful to live with an irascible drunk who will never admit he's wrong—and that's just what you get with literary types who have climbed the ladder of language to rarefied levels of rationalized behavior.

One writer I stayed with was a tall Texan who prowled around in his Stetson hat and boxer shorts, and who drank a fifth of Jack Daniel's a day. We sublet a nice big house together, and kept a thirteen-year-old dog for the traveling owners. The dog was an obese, blind, tumor-ridden miniature poodle who wandered through the house like a slow-moving bowling ball with hair. My roommate would go into shrieking rages on the phone with his estranged wife, pummel the couch with his fists, and generally menace the place by careening drunkenly about. I came to live in terror that he would step on the dog. I was fearful that he would start punching holes in the walls, which I knew from his reminiscences that he liked to do.

It was a real concession for him just to punch the couch. It wasn't satisfying, and over the weeks I could tell he was going to go for the hollow paneling the first chance he got. Late at night, when he was at his worst, the only way I could be sure of protecting the sublet walls was to get him to read long chapters from his latest doomed novel until he collapsed. Finally, he got a wall anyway, in a closet when I wasn't home.

In the end, the dog lived and the owners didn't discover the holes in the closet. They did report a little mold in one of the bathrooms—mine, of course.

So there is nothing left for me except to live with strangers. The ways you come to live with a stranger vary; some people might not be able to do it at all, but for me it has always been easy. Once, in a grocery store parking lot, I was invited to stay in a mobile home with an elderly couple who wanted to hypnotize me so I would make up with my wife.

More commonly, though, I am invited into the house of a perfect stranger because I am a writer. In this sense, I am my own bait. There are a lot of strangers out there with stories in them, and they need somebody like me to help them whip their diamonds in the rough into shape to be jetted off for publication. Most writers wouldn't be caught dead fooling with these people, but when I'm on the skids I'll do anything. It's eerie, but the word gets out when I'm available. There seems to be effective networking among eccentric would-be writers, especially the ones who go to those workshops where I teach, and if I'm on the street almost all I have to do is wait by a phone booth for someone to call.

In this way, I have come to live with an international dope smuggler. I have lived with a prize-winning raiser of camellias. I have lived with a teacher of poultry science. I have lived with a psychologist who made me promise that if he went crazy I would get him over into Oklahoma where nobody would notice.

I have lived with the rich and the poor, and I need to take a moment to point out the relativity of money in this context. Luxury is wonderful, all right, but at these times it's also a reminder of my own impoverished state.

It's a dismal admission, but left alone amongst plenty, I begin to live like an animal. Just let my rich host leave town. I'll never make my bed again or hang up my clothes, and I like to leave wet towels on the bathroom floor. I prowl around undressed and unshaved and allow cartoons to play on the TV. I smirk at the herbal tea and jars of button mushrooms, and I like to let my empty Spam and Budweiser cans pile up in the gourmet's kitchen.

On the other hand, in the house of a bum I can be a paragon of a guest. The awful truth is that it gives me something to look down on when I most need it. I tend to clean up and lend order and buy needed things for the home. In general, I create the impression that even though I may be momentarily shipwrecked on my own emotional shore, I can still elevate the quality of life in this pitiful dump I've landed in.

In either situation, I'm a beast. I'm even worse than, say, the golden retriever I left behind, because while a dog may be nosy in a curious sort of way, he isn't known to be all that critical about what he finds. Also, a dog at least seems to know who he is. Homeless souls don't seem to know who they are at all, and are always looking for clues in other people's mirrors or, worse, their closets and chests-of-drawers.

I can justify living in other people's houses. I can say that I am learning how the other half lives, that I am among *source* people (another good reason to stay away from other writers), and while it's true, it's beside the point. The essential message I have returned with to share with you is this: While I acknowledge aberrancy in relatives and avoid them like the plague, I fear that out there, in the sanctum of their own homes, is a *whole nation* of lunatics.

Every time I move in with a stranger, I tell myself it will be the last. The last time I did it—more recently than I care to admit—was far from the worst, but because it is current it stands out. In some ways, it even was one of my more successful stays in other people's houses. . . .

As always, just when I needed it, I got an offer over the phone. A nice-sounding fellow told me he had made his fortune acquiring land for an oil company, but had residual problems to do with having been tortured by the Chinese; the problems, though vague to me, had caused him to retire at fifty-one, a wealthy but unhappy man. He had spent the last few years fishing on his private lake and writing a book about being brainwashed, not once but twice—first by the Chinese then again by our very own Veterans Administration. I agreed to move in with him and his wife, where I could live in luxury and also be paid handsomely to critique his book.

Jerry Joe and Stella turned out to be good country people with a collection of *Reader's Digest*s that went back twenty years. An American flag flew outside, and this grand country estate was comfortably filled with gimcracks from Stuckey's, pictures of doe-eyed children sniffing daisies, and diplomas from institutions such as The School of Hard Knocks and the Texas Fishing Academy.

But looks can be deceiving, and right away things began to happen. "Stella's sister is going to be here, too, I'm afraid," Jerry Joe said. "The poor thing's been through hell. Her boy's a killer locked up at Huntsville. Her husband died three months ago, and she just had shock treatments." He paused and said cryptically, "I don't know. Sometimes I think those treatments do more harm than good."

The sister turned out to be a raw-boned country woman about sixty-five. She weighed over two hundred pounds, looked tough as nails, and turned out to be a sort of modern day Ma Barker. The same day I showed up, she arrived with a U-Haul truck full of, I heard later, hot merchandise she planned to sell to help with her killer offspring's appeal.

I was assigned to a nice big bedroom with a private bath, a built-in desk, and a TV in the wall with a remote switch beside my bed. It was a perfectly good bed, but before I even got unpacked it was removed by two long-haired, pop-eyed movers and replaced with a king-sized Serta Perfect Sleeper off the U-Haul. Also, a Wang word processor with a display screen and printer was left on my desk. Jerry Joe came in, looking sheepish. "Humor poor Sister," he said.

I gazed at the Wang and thought that I probably could humor her, all right. But then I heard a great bray from the den, and language foul enough to shock even me, a man so jaded he might soon be sleeping in alleys and consorting with harlots. "She's on this medicine," Jerry Joe said sadly. "It makes her talk like that."

After that, I huddled in my room, pretending to work, but finally it was time to have a drink and I needed ice. I held off till halfway through Dan Rather, then made a dash for the kitchen. As I passed through the den, Sister was in the middle of yet another filthy joke. She stopped talking as I went by, then stopped again as I came back through with my bucket of ice. I heard her say behind me: "Is he married or what?"

"Separated," Stella said.

"He better watch it," Sister said and brayed. "I haven't had a man in three months and I walk in my sleep."

Later I was invited to play cards with the family, but declined, saying that I had to work—a line writers can use to wonderful advantage. It makes non-writing cardplayers feel guilty and gives writers privacy to watch television.

As long as I had the TV on, I didn't hear much, but when I turned it off to go to sleep, I could hear Sister again. "Does he work all the time?" she asked around midnight. I went to sleep, I think, but only for a little before I heard my doorknob turning. Light came through a widening crack, then the door shut. "Hell, he's asleep!" Sister yelled.

I sprang up and turned the lock, and when she discovered *that* she began butting against the door. I quaked in bed, hoping Jerry Joe would save me. But it was Stella who caught her, and a loud argument started out in the hall.

Finally, I let Jerry Joe in. "We never should've brought that bed in here," he panted. "It's her dead husband's bed, and now she says she wants in it."

I was prepared to turn the bed over to her and sleep in my car, if it would do any good, but before much longer the yelling began to die down. It flared up a few times over the course of an hour, then Sister just seemed to run out of steam. I heard her say she was tired and going to sleep, which she apparently did because I didn't hear another sound all night.

Next morning over coffee, Jerry Joe said, "I'm worried. Sister's picked too much cotton to give up like she did last night. I'm taking her for a checkup." Later he drove off to the hospital with Sister and came home without her. "I was right," he said. "She's got leukemia, poor old thing." Jerry Joe cleared his throat and shook his head. "Well, anyway, now maybe we can get some work done."

I really liked this Jerry Joe and felt bad that the Chinese and especially the VA had treated him the way they had. His story was worth telling, all right, but my nerves were too shot to help him. I stayed the day, but that evening I crept out and checked into a Holiday Inn at forty bucks a night. The price was a little steep, but in all my days as a homeless soul I've never been happier than I was in that room, free at last to be my own miserable self.

What I Really Think about Pigeons

Coming out of yet another divorce, this time into a herpes-ridden world, I decided to keep to myself for a bit, just read good books and wait for a change in the weather.

I had just left heaven on earth in Texas to live in Columbus, Ohio. Why anyone makes such a move is always the same; we want to make a living so we won't starve and die. Anyway, James Thurber and Philip Roth had lived in Columbus, for a while, and I meant to make the best of it for a while, too.

I considered an A-frame in the woods in Hocking County, away from the city, but it seemed a little *too* removed. After all, it wasn't that I didn't want to be close to people. I just didn't want to talk to them very much—and I certainly didn't want to touch them until I saw if medical science, which can't even cure baldness, was going to get something done about the latest scourge on suffering humanity.

So I got a real deal on a garret atop a charming brick building in a restored, historic, and urban part of town called German Village. Part of the appeal of this attic apartment was that it had a rear entrance impossible to find by anybody except perhaps a lost meter reader.

No matter if gaudy, tactless tourists off buses tried to barge into the apartment downstairs. No matter if I suspected that prostitutes and heroin addicts shared the building. No matter if couples of various sexual preferences had shrieking fights in the streets below after the bars closed. I was in the cool pink center of Columbus activity, yet above it all. I could see but not be seen. I was blessedly alone.

In short, I had reached precisely the level of the pigeon. I discovered this right away, at daybreak, when they began their mating rituals on the air conditioner by my head. Anyone living alone can come to resent the sound of sex. Pigeon sex is especially odious to listen to, and I soon grew to think of my nearest companions as lice-infested morons. Though I had kept pigeons as a child, I now disliked the way the great bull males puffed up their chests and urgently did those gurgling pirouettes. And I was annoyed to see how well it worked for them—how after a certain amount of time the drab, meek, but equally infested females always succumbed, squatting and quivering in helpless submission.

A recently divorced man living alone in an attic is, I think, generally moody and looking for something to take out his misery on. This is a bad time for him to have pets, for he will only see their fleas. Even a goldfish in a bowl may gall him with its little jerky movements. Such a man may actively seek out mice or water bugs or anything else in an attic that is socially acceptable for him to murder. Yet in the middle of his depravity, he may unexpectedly come upon a mouse in a skillet and be oddly touched by it, thinking of it as one of God's special little creatures and a pal.

One day I went into my kitchen, a room I had to stoop to be in, and looked for this or that to eat cold out of a can. I surprised a female pigeon on the other side of the window. She didn't fly away, but uneasily peered at me, obviously wishing I would go down on the street with the rest of humankind. They don't like people, I observed. But they need us in the way that, say, a rat or roach needs us. I drew a parallel between the first pigeons who lived in holes in the sides of cliffs and their descendants who now have such an affinity for German Village. The volume of pigeon crap here is alarming, and I could imagine this whole part of town eventually being buried in it—giving future archaeologists something to unearth, and perhaps leading them to ponder how we ever let ourselves in for a fate worse than Pompeii's.

The female pigeon squatted and laid an egg which fell to the sidewalk three stories below. This stirred love feelings in her mate, who began to gurgle urgently. Pigeons may be our closest bird counterparts, I thought. After all, they do love their little homes. They marry for life. They share their little domestic duties. They also philander and abuse their children. And more than one jealous pigeon husband has been known to batter his wife for wandering too far from the nest. . . .

A recently divorced man is in real trouble if he teaches at a university and is off duty because it is summer or one of a generous number of other university holidays. He could use his free time to wonderful advantage, but he won't. He had rather sit and do nothing so he can see the future as drab and pointless, and the past as golden and lost.

While I spent my days mulling half a lifetime of golden moments, I recalled that when I was twelve and briefly raised pigeons I had felt only fascination for them. White Kings were my specialty. They were gentle, decent birds, pure as Ivory Snow, and they made love in the privacy of their nest box. I adored my White King pets and rode my bicycle around strange neighborhoods with two of them perched on my handle bars and one on my rear fender. I was, I hoped, creating a certain mystique about myself—and I probably was, too.

Pigeons have impressive genetic plasticity, like dogs, and can be bred to almost any shape, size, color, and function. I remember seeing in a giant pigeon book some glorious color pictures of exotic, grotesque breeds. One had a head that seemed to be all wattle and shaped like a spool of thread. Another had a breast so large that she couldn't see over it; her little head seemed to grow out of the middle of her back.

From an ad in the paper, I came to know a man in the country near Dallas who bred birds called Parlor Pigeons. They had been bred to the point that they couldn't fly, but they loved to turn backward somersaults over and over again.

Also on his farm, I remember seeing pigeon acrobatics high overhead in the wide Texas skies. The birds were called Rollers and Tumblers because those were the tricks they did up there, both alone and in flocks. The Tumblers would go up almost out of sight, then plummet, tumbling over and over and pulling out of their dives at the last second. Some actually crashed, the man said, but I never saw it happen.

As I educated myself about pigeons, I was especially taken with stories of the great pigeon heroes of both world wars—messenger pigeons with names like the Burma Queen, Jungle Joe, and Cher Ami—who gave their lives to save our boys and who now are on display in museums, stuffed, of course. I loved the peacetime story of the pigeon who carried piggyback a singing canary named Tessie Testpilot from New Jersey to New York. In just twenty minutes, Tessie— nestled inside a special canary carrier—was delivered to her new owner, a poor crippled girl in the hospital.

But most of all, I was struck with their instinctive ability to get home from almost any distance. It is a feat that has always filled us with wonder. Some researchers believe that a pigeon in the middle of the continent can, in a sense, "hear" both of the great oceans at one time. Then there are scientists who think that a homing pigeon, having traveled six hundred or more miles, can find a certain air conditioner in German Village just by its particular magnetic convolutions.

A recently divorced man will hole up for a while, if he's smart, then carefully venture out again. Some divorce experts say that you should live alone for two or three years before remarrying. They don't say how long to hide in an attic, but I suggest about one week. I stayed a little longer, but got nothing out of the last few days. By one week I had begun feeding bread to my feathered companions, putting bite-sized pieces along the kitchen window sill. But I never did adjust to the noise in the morning, and couldn't seem to decide whether to move my bed or my air conditioner. Either way, I lost, and sometimes it made me just hate their little guts.

Then early one evening in midsummer, as the sun

set behind the ivy-covered brick buildings, I descended to the level of my fellow humans and strolled along the German Village streets. Joggers were still out, but couples were beginning to walk to the neighborhood restaurants and bars and outdoor cafes. On this evening, at any rate, it all seemed pleasantly civilized. Maybe it was just getting out of that attic, but I suddenly felt good about being in the Midwest, between the two great oceans. I wasn't able to hear them, of course, but I knew where they were anyway, in ways we humans have for knowing things that in other creatures can seem so full of mystery.

Living with Crumbsnatchers

For a while, my new friend seemed to think I wouldn't hang around long because she had a couple of kids, and there was a chance of that all right. I had spent half a lifetime believing that children and writing don't go together, and I had stuck to it, too. So for weeks now I had feared I was on the verge of making a terrible mistake. If I had given up having my own little bundles of joy in the name of literature, why should I suddenly pick up somebody else's extra luggage?

I couldn't tell if I was being brutal or just realistic, but mainly I didn't want to ruin what little chance I had left to make it in the world of books, didn't want people to shake their heads and say, "If he had only waited."

Then one day my friend took me aback. "What are you so worried about?" she said. "I wouldn't even consider marrying you. At least not till I see if the four of us can get along."

I was indignant. "I have to woo the crumbsnatchers, too?" I asked, dredging up a pejorative from my Texas past designed to keep kids somewhere around the level of the ant.

She explained: "If we all aren't happy, you won't be happy. And with your record I don't want to take any chances. I don't want another divorce."

I began to soften up. I began looking at the crumbsnatchers with a paternal eye. But when people who really know me found out what was going on, they blanched. They wouldn't tell me why, exactly, but one did say, "Some people just aren't cut out to have children."

As I tried to get to know these kids, I found out that they didn't even like me—a real blow. "They just need a while to get used to you," their mother said, and suggested I move in for three-day weekends to see if I could crack the ice.

I agreed and packed my bag to give it a try. "Have I gone crazy?" I asked an old friend and father of two himself. "I think so," he said. "But it'll be good for you to get a taste of what the rest of us go through." Another implored me at least not to try to be their father. "You don't have the right," he said. "It's a violation of their space."

The weekends were my precious writing time, and right away I could tell I was in for trouble. In that house nothing was sacred. Privacy was out. There were no closed doors anywhere. What bed they landed in seemed to be at random. The room I wanted to use for writing was air-conditioned—the reason I wanted it—and great shrieks went up the moment I tried to keep anybody out. Give it time, I thought. I decided to go a few days without writing to try to make things work.

On the first day of our first weekend I studied the kids like specimens and came to some preliminary conclusions. The pubescent daughter was too nice; she seemed two-faced, and it turned out she was. Her mother reported that she was talking behind my back, saying that I dressed like a bum. The boy, who was ten, either ignored me or was rude. Then without warning he would regress, crawl in his mother's lap, suck his thumb, and whine.

I decided the girl's problems were too subtle to cope with, and anyway she wasn't giving me any trouble, so I focused on the boy. At least with him what you saw was what you got. I remembered that at his age I was the mad bomber of the neighborhood, and a sadistic practical joker as well, so I told him all about my exploits. About the experiments we did on cats in the name of science. The dirt we poured into the gas tank of a cranky neighbor's car. The little self-exploding firecrackers we tried to drop by kite on the old shrew across the alley.

He cackled and told me of his own evil plan to send the spoiled little girl next door down roller-coaster hill in his stolen shopping cart—or else just throw up on her.

Then he wanted to toss the football, which I was afraid to try because of the pinched nerve in my neck. But I remembered that I used to be good with a Frisbee and thought I could handle that, pinched nerve or not. I was pleased to see that the boy was terrible at it.

After an exhilarating hour of watching him drop his Frisbee, I decided to take him to Hobbyland after an airplane, and to my wonder it made the girl jealous. When she sulkily got in the car to go along, I felt

I was making headway with her as well.

That night, as a rejoinder when they both beat me at their video games, I challenged them to be creative for a change. I proposed getting some video equipment and making a movie of our own. They agreed and for an hour we brainstormed over a possible script like one of the more sickening Monty Python movies. I was shocked by the violence in their young hearts and their prurient view of human anatomy—but was awed by their associative abilities and black humor. They just need direction, I thought. Then it dawned on me what work I would be getting into, and I secretly hoped they would lose interest.

Next day, the kids and I spent the morning target practicing with the BB gun of my youth, then God help me, I took them to see *Twilight Zone—The Movie*. They loved that pandering piece of juvenilia, and as they shrieked and squealed and tittered, I felt I had pitched my fate with morons. Then I remembered that taste, after all, is cultivated, and I forgave their ingenuous souls for not having been on earth as long as I have.

That was a big step forward for me, and they somehow seemed to have perceived it. Afterward, when I cooked hamburgers and hot dogs on the grill, they became my slaves, vying for who could scurry to the house for any little thing, and I began to plot other ways to harness all that squandered energy.

Meanwhile, without having to cook or spend every minute with her kids, their mother used the time to get some writing done herself. She didn't hesitate to yell down for her live-in critic every five minutes, either, but for some reason I didn't care. I felt good. Healthy. Youthful.

On Sunday, the boy improved his Frisbee performance, and I felt proud of him. He said he wanted me to play the part of Captain Gore, the starring role in our proposed movie, which touched me enough to want to go through with it after all. The girl, to my amazement, was following me around like a duck. For the moment, anyway, she had developed a real crush and took three showers that day so she could make those daring, giggling teenage dashes in a towel.

I seemed to be watching evolution in miniature. They had gone from ape to human in a single weekend. "We'll pass you if you'll pass us," the girl said out of nowhere, and I realized how savvy they were about our weekend experiment.

Deep down, I now suspected that they were smarter than me—but then my own intellectual level seemed to have dropped like a stone. I felt in a constant frenzy. I saw humor in anything. Against the rules, I said we could fly our new model airplane in the house. Then I instigated a pillow fight.

After the kids were in bed that night, their mother and I critiqued the weekend. When she said she felt fine about it, I said, "So what are we waiting for?" "A lot," she said. "Kids are easy to win over, but believe me it doesn't last." She wanted to test my staying power once things got rough. If we all could survive about six more months of these three-day weekends, she thought she'd be convinced.

So I'm over at their place every weekend now, and I haven't written a word except to jot down clever things that the kids say and do. But the real issue is that I hardly see their mother any more at all. While I'm out in the backyard rehearsing in my new Captain Gore cap, she's in the air-conditioned room for days at a time, writing like the devil. I was better off when we were dating. At the same time, though, I really am crazy about the crumbsnatchers—enough to consider being a single parent if I had the chance, even if it meant going down in history as a balding Erma Bombeck with whiskers.

Life in the Doghouse

The only thing I didn't like about my new place in the Ohio countryside was the doghouse. I hadn't met the previous owner, so I don't know what had lived in that doghouse, but it had been staked beside the house on a great chain—still there—and I thought the beast must have paced incessantly, because there was a bald spot thirty feet in diameter around the house, as if a flying saucer had landed and baked the ground with alien energy.

The doghouse itself was big enough for me to curl up inside, though I never would have of course, and was covered from top to bottom with brown asphalt roofing shingles. Unlike most doghouses, it wasn't a miniature of a human house, nor did it have any other architectural qualities to make it interesting to look at. It was square, with rounded corners formed by overlapping tarpaper and shingles, which somehow gave it an even more unpleasant and indomitable look.

The couple of acres was a paradise for me, a sylvan setting, except for this blight, so the day after I moved in, I went out to tear it down. Right away, I saw it was going to be more difficult than I had thought. There was no easy way to get at it. The abrasive roofing shingle surface was discouraging to me, in the way that crawling around on the roof of a human house is somehow discouraging.

Also, I had the feeling that there was something inside. The doorway was the only place to hold on to, but I thought I would be taking a chance to wrap my fingers around the inside of the door frame. It was dark in there, too, so I got a flashlight. To use it involved getting on my knees and putting my face right up to the opening.

There was a snake in the doghouse. It was large and looked black, and it wasn't asleep. It was coiled up, with its head sticking out of the center of the coils, smelling me with its tongue.

I got a rake and dragged the snake out onto the bald spot of ground, where it quickly coiled up again, hissed, and struck at the rake. I was new to this part of the country and didn't know my snakes yet; I didn't want to kill it if it was harmless, so I went in the house and waited for it to go away. It outwaited me, though, nestled by the door of the doghouse, and finally I dragged it back into the open with the rake, got my axe, and chopped it in half.

I wondered about the dog's master, and why he had wanted to construct a doghouse that I couldn't turn over. No dog of this earth ever needed a doghouse like that. If the master had overmade it out of hubris, say, why had he made it so awful to look at?

I think it must have weighed six hundred pounds. I didn't yet have proper tools for country living, so instead of a sledgehammer, I used an unwieldy maul.

Instead of a crowbar, I used a tire tool, the bent-rod
kind that doesn't change tires very well either. At first,
all I could do was hit around the vulnerable doorway
with the maul, then prize at the opening with the tire
tool. Eventually, the front wall began to loosen. I
removed the asphalt shingles and tarpaper that were
wrapped around the front corners, and found seams
where the front was nailed to the rest of the doghouse. With the tire tool, I was able to pry off the
entire front at once.

Some friends from the city had been watching out
a window. They took a break from helping unpack
boxes and came out for a close look at what I had
done—then they hurried back, preferring to be inside
away from the bugs.

I now was able to see clearly the construction. All
sides had an inside and outside wall, with heavy plastic
insulation in between, and had tenpenny nails every
few inches connecting the sides to a sturdy two-by-
four frame. I was in a weakened state from taking the
front off, and the sun was getting hot, and all I could
do was swing my maul around on the inside of the
doghouse and pummel the walls. There wasn't enough
room, and I kept knocking the pipe handle against
the corners and hurting my hands from the shock,
but I still made headway.

The north wall was the first to fall, and as I sat
panting on the ground beside my maul, I became
aware of vague movement around the open ends of
the remaining sides. But when I got up to look, all
that remained were some giant amber-colored ants
on the ground, carrying fat white eggs. They were
reeling under their loads, and seemed consternated,
but as I watched they began to find their way. Or

perhaps one found his way and showed the others, but at any rate they were quickly out of sight beneath the doghouse.

With a second wall down, I had a clear line of attack with my maul, and hit the doghouse with one satisfying blow after another. With long nails, plastic, asphalt, and tarpaper all connecting everything to everything else, the house clung to itself and nothing fell without a struggle.

Whenever a wall went down, there was a last-ditch lunge for life by inhabitants of the doghouse—mostly small bugs, but there were centipedes in there, too, as well as frogs or toads, and a lot of crickets.

Where the family of field mice came from, I'm not sure, unless it was under the floor, but in any case the father was a big brown decisive fellow who sprang out and barreled for the creek without looking back. But Mrs. Mouse and her three children stood blinking in the sun, dazed. They didn't run the way I thought they should, but moved carefully and seemed in wonder. They looked extraordinarily clean, with delicate pink skin and fine fur that was a light gray on top and white beneath. Their little sides heaved in and out. Finally, they found some way back into whatever remained of their home.

But when the last wall fell and I moved it to try to make a neater pile, I saw Mrs. Mouse and her children crushed on the ground.

The dismembered doghouse made quite a pile, and my success with it inspired me to attack the thirty-foot bald spot with my rake. I hardly made a scratch in the packed, baked earth. The garden hose was at the front of the house and wouldn't reach around, so I couldn't water down the spot, either. I decided to have a roto-tiller person come out, plow it up, and plant grass seed, but before I got around to it, I found myself using the bald spot as a place to pile yet more trash.

It was a good place for me to drag the limbs I was pruning from all the maple trees; they provided a nat-ural-looking cover for the spot, and I temporarily had a place to take them. A couple of days after the fall of the doghouse, as I was adding to my pile with yet more limbs, I noticed the two smelly fly-covered halves of the snake I had killed. They were moving toward the creek, along with the mice, who seemed to be going after their husband and father.

I investigated and found that a gang of loathsome-looking gray bugs were carrying the carcasses to a point beyond the perimeter of hard ground, where they then began to dig graves to put them in. They worked together like a road gang, and I was told that they are called burying beetles. They were hiding the corpses from other scavengers, and would dig back down in the graves to snack at their leisure.

I added to my pile of limbs throughout the summer and into the autumn, enjoying how easy it was to prune a tree limb with a small, inexpensive pruning saw. It's not even very hard to cut down a whole medium-sized tree, but getting rid of what you've cut is another matter. Even though my ever-mounting pile ultimately was just unfinished work, it was an impressive sight, and I began to take naive pride in its size.

Creatures began to live in the pile of dead limbs—chipmunks especially, though birds seemed drawn to it for some reason as well. I worried about snakes being somewhere in there, though as it turned out I had

murdered a harmless chicken snake that day. It was
a wet fall, and toward November I decided it would
be safe to burn the pile, though a little at a time, which
would mean making another smaller pile nearby and
feeding it from the larger one.

I invited a half dozen of my city friends out to help.
A bonfire in autumn creates a festive mood that verges
on abandon. The pile took till after midnight to burn,
then we came upon the flattened sides of the doghouse. My usually mild-mannered friends were caught
up in the joy of burning and cried out in glee at the
sight of those substantial walls.

Once we had carried the first one-hundred-pound
section over and heaved it onto the blaze, nuts from
the surrounding trees began to fall like little bombs,
shaken loose by the rising heat. What had been a
cheery blaze of burning maple turned into an unnat-
ural-looking inferno. The smoke was black from the
burning asphalt and plastic, and the air full of little
flakes of ash that wouldn't seem to go away.

Then I flushed out a snake. It was a small one who
seemed eager to get to the creek, so I ushered it along
with my rake and let it live. But a friend was certain
from my description that I had ushered off a copper-
head, and some of our abandon went away. In the
dark woods and among the flames and sparks and
swirling smoke, we could see copperheads everywhere.

We finally came to the last wall of the doghouse,
and once I had raised it and balanced it on one edge,
I looked beneath where it had been. Strange dark shiny
creatures slithered and writhed like worms over the
wet ground. I thought that they were young copperheads, but then I saw they had little legs and some-

body said that they were salamanders.

It seemed as if they had come from nothing under the wrecked doghouse during the course of the rainy autumn, but they must have crawled up from the creek, some of them so small that they hardly seemed to have legs at all.

Only one of my friends had seen a salamander before in person, but among the group certain things were known. The courtship of salamanders is complex, like that of ritualistic birds, with swaying bodies and bobbing heads, and even little squeaking noises. If you touch an especially slimy species, the coating on their skin will stick to your fingers and not easily come off. They are not poisonous. Before the age of reason, it was thought that you could throw one in a fire and it would not burn.

Why these salamanders of different ages all came from the creek to live beneath the doghouse, no one was sure. I wondered why any of the house's creatures would have wanted to live there, but they had all seemed happy enough until I arrived.

In any case, the purging was now complete. The dog beast and his mysterious master were only flecks of ash in the black night. Life seemed as free of evil to my friends and me as when it first crawled from the antediluvian slime.

Epilogue:
The Truth at Last

I'm escaping at least part of one of the worst winters in Ohio history by staying with my old biologist friend Eddie, who lives in a small Texas city on the Gulf Coast. I find myself spending much of the day basking in the sunshine in his backyard and holding a pen and legal pad so the passing meter men will think I'm doing something productive. But I keep an eye on the time, too, because around three in the afternoon the day really takes a turn.

In the week or so since I arrived, Eddie and I have developed a wonderful ritual. While his wife and kids are off at work and school, he and I watch old movies on his VCR for a few hours every afternoon. It's a nice break from my writing—which I really do work at, sort of—and from his study of fish heads as he prepares to teach next semester's biology classes at the local college.

We like the old creature features best, corny as they are. Even after all these years, the childlike scientist in me still likes all the paraphernalia in the evil laboratories. The mordant dreamer in Eddie (which I'm noticing more of all the time) likes the allegorical quality of blood-sucking and other charming aspects of the concept of the undead. Eddie and I have known one another since the ninth grade. As teenagers, when we introduced our different interests and natures to one another, it seems to have caused some lasting hybrid crossover. You might think that becoming both analytical and conceptual would allow you to do almost anything easily and well. But looking at us loafing like this in midday, I think we may have shared only enough of our qualities to have thrown us off the straight and narrow course to greatness.

These creature features we watch make me hark back to one night thirty years ago when we did something especially grisly in the name of science. I am haunted by what happened that night, and I know I will take the memory to my grave, the way I will take along the beatific face of my blessed grandmother. What I can't forget is the sight of a freshly—though crudely—extracted cat brain, the size of a walnut, floating in a fishbowl full of alcohol. Two wires, red and green, had been stuck in the brain and hooked up to a car battery placed beside the bowl. Our idea—Eddie's actually—was that the electrical current might well keep the brain alive. If it worked, it meant that at fifteen years of age we had found the key to immortality, or at least were hot on truth's trail.

The little brain didn't look alive to me, but then I wasn't the expert either. "What do you think?" I asked Eddie. Eddie studied the brain, then glanced at his watch. "I think we kept it alive for a little bit," he said.

Looking back, I know of course that we didn't.

Worse, I think that Eddie knew it even at the time. The only truth around that night wasn't in the fish-bowl—it was in the fact that two misguided teenagers had looked for meaning in a poor dead cat's head instead of in their own.

My perception of myself is that I grow more and more adjusted with age. I might even like to have children someday. Eddie, on the other hand, seems to become more and more eccentric. He follows a well-beaten path from home to school where he discusses the anatomy of fish heads with all-female classes of aspiring nurses. Then there is a certain store he visits to buy crickets to feed his pet scorpions. He busies himself with grant proposals to go to far-flung places after frogs. Then he hangs bat-like in his study on a homemade contraption not nearly so conventional or socially acceptable as my inversion table.

And that's about it, except now for our afternoon matinees and late-night talks about the natural world. You have to understand that I don't usually live like this. I drink. I consort. I send things by Zap Mail. So staying down here with Eddie, without a car, I have to be ever-alert for his trips after crickets, so I can get to the Piggly-Wiggly supermarket and buy white wine.

The other day a notable thing happened at Piggly-Wiggly. As I stood in the checkout line, a busy-looking fellow snatched some dated *Reader's Digest*s from under my nose and put fresh ones in their place, the way you do produce. I looked and, sure enough, something I had written was in the magazine. It was a nature-related piece, so I bought two copies and gave one to Eddie, who took it home and read it. Then late that night he emerged from his study to take issue with some of my details.

Eddie's main quibble was this. When I lived in Cedar Hill, I wanted to know all I could about the area, so I read everything I could and checked with the old-timers, and emerged with a pleasant sense of the place, past and present.

Of all the stories I heard, I was most struck by this one. Twenty-four hours after a tornado wiped the little town off the map in the late 1800s, it was reported that a hay fork fell out of a clear blue sky and stuck up in the ground. (A bolt of cloth supposedly fell as well.) Now, I was baffled by the story. The only thing I could think was that the items got up in a jet stream and swirled around all that time, then plummeted. The fact was, everybody I talked to knew about the bizarre incident and swore it was true. They couldn't explain it. They were baffled, too, but *they knew it had happened.* That was good enough for me, and I wrote about it as a baffling fact.

The scientist in Eddie was amused by my gullibility. He said that the only way that hay fork could have fallen to the ground twenty-four hours later was for it to have been stuck in a tree all that time, then just dropped loose on its own (along with, he supposed, the bolt of cloth). He easily dismissed as hearsay the honorable word of all those respectable people.

I have the sinking feeling that Eddie and his hard-nosed approach may be right. I have utter respect for the scientists—I'm just not one of them. I'm snagged somewhere between scientists and my ex-wife. I want to believe that the hay fork incident really happened, *for reasons not yet understood by science.*

I wish the whole issue of truth would just shut up and go away. Probably I don't want truth at all. Probably at this point I just write out of habit. Probably all I really want in life is to come up with a good story, have a few drinks, and get a good night's sleep.

I think that there is something about sitting in Texas sunshine in winter, completely alone except for a six-week-old cat perched on my shoulder like a little screech owl, that makes me oddly irascible, like the misanthropic hermit I'm probably destined to be. When I say that I grow more adjusted with age and that Eddie grows more eccentric, I know that I am suspect. And I should be, because in truth I think Eddie is a paragon of sanity compared to the world at large. What I have adjusted to, of course, is not to the world but to myself.

The way I relate to the world these days, as much as possible, is by words on paper. I've never understood writers who say that they would write even if they lived on a deserted island with no hope at all of ever being read. I can understand writing a journal, say, or even poetry as a way to reflect yourself on paper to know that you still exist and what, if anything, you think.

But for me there need to be readers. I need to know that communication has taken place. And the way I find that out, for sure, is to hear from a reader. The predictable way is by letter, either directly or by way of a magazine I've appeared in. But there is also the telephone, word of mouth, and—though I've not personally experienced this—burning crosses in the yard. There is a dichotomy here. I want reader reaction—but their reactions have convinced me the world is mad, or at least the part of it that writes letters to writers and their editors.

I've adjusted, more or less, but at first the letters were alarming. For years after I wrote about a mass murderer, I got letters from criminals wanting their stories told, too; some wanted to marry the ex-girl-friend of my mass murderer. I write about nature and am attacked for not writing about urban blight. I attack people who live off other people's baldness and get discount offers for wigs and transplants. I puzzle over knots and get unreadable treatises on the theory of surfaces. I dream up a character called the Cat Woman of Cedar Hill, and a reader does a city-wide search so that she can report to me that such a person doesn't exist. A man on a plane writes to tell me that owls in his neighborhood are flying off with domesticated cats. A retired grade school teacher reports from out of nowhere about the pecking order of milk cows. . . .

The other night, Eddie asked me a sensitive question, though it came across as more of a statement: "You lie sometimes, don't you?" Of course, I told him. I lie like a dog, especially in matters of pride or vanity or weakness such as hair loss or drinking or work habits. I finished by saying that he does too. Then he closed in: "There never was a fire in your birdbath, was there?"

The truth is that a lot of letters I get—justifiable ones from people who probably are saner than I'll ever be—address that issue. Undeniably, there is for me something perversely satisfying about lying to thousands or occasionally millions of people, but these days my lies are almost always ones of omission. A penguin did bite my hand one hot day in Dallas. There was a fire in my birdbath. It's the context surrounding such events that I leave out, and context apparently is what people want, because whenever it's missing they write letters to my editors, trying to get me in trouble.

I still embellish as much as the next familiar essayist, I guess, but I haven't told any real lies to speak of since 1972 when I got caught at it. It had to do with the nightmarish trip to El Salvador that Eddie got me into in 1971. In the chronicle I wrote afterward, I said that the Guatemalan border guards thought our electric razor was a transmitter en route to the guerrillas. When I committed the falsehood, I didn't think that much about it. I was trying to be funny, I guess, but probably I also wanted to get even with those border guards for making us unload.

It was just a couple of lines, and might not have been noticed, except that when the piece appeared in the *New York Times* the paper singled out my fabrication, using it as a caption for a giant illustration on the front page of the travel section.

This is a testament to the power of lying, I think, because what I wrote practically caused an international incident. Over fifty articles were written in Spanish denouncing the *New York Times* and the gringo Allen. The president of Guatemala made a speech to his country saying, "First the Pentagon Papers and now this!" One especially irate journalist referred to me as "hyena meat à la *New York Times*." Guatemala threatened to cancel travel advertising with the *Times*, and for weeks I lived in terror that, between the *Times* and the Guatemalans, someone was going to get me but good.

It was a tempest in a teapot, all right, and it blew over, but even today when I fly to Costa Rica—my idea of heaven on earth—I pray the plane doesn't go down over Guatemala.

The cat on my shoulder is nine weeks old now, and I have done all the brooding about truth that I ever intend to, except somehow to draw a conclusion. It is getting cold even in Texas, but if it weren't, I'd still have to go home to Ohio to tell students things like: "Don't lie unless you're sure you can get away with it."

A CONCLUSION

On the day Eddie took me to the airport, he and I swung by the college so he could show me around his well-equipped laboratory. Among other things, I looked at his gallstone collection, which he likes to rearrange every now and then. After we had fed crickets to his giant black scorpions from Veracruz, he took a bottle off a shelf and handed it to me. Floating in there—sort of like that cat brain from our past— was a tiny tail. It was a human tail. "They're more common than you think," Eddie said. "They're usually just surgically removed at birth and thrown away." He stared at the floating tail and said in a sort of cosmic tone: "Everything there is to know probably is in that bottle."

I stared at the tail, too. It was a stark reminder of where we had come from, all right. I wouldn't want to have it around to ponder on a daily basis. But it was a pleasant affirmation of how far we've come, too. It all balanced out, I decided, and I left for Ohio feeling good for Eddie having shared his little bottled tail with me.

DATE DUE			